STORM SOAKED STRANGERS

Sierra Prynne

A *Dark Encounters* Novella

CHAPTER 1

I don't need this to end with happily ever after. This is a scene I've paid good money for. One I've been fantasizing about for months ever since I learned of The Company's existence.

The Company.

It sounds like the sort of place they'd joke about in a self-aware office sitcom. A made-up corporation that sells hot air or staples or something.

But the jokey vibe wore off around the time I was putting in my application. It's members only and you must be nominated by someone who's already a member to even be considered. The vetting process requires a physical and bloodwork, a background check, and unfettered access to your computer. And that's all before the *lengthy* questionnaire you have to fill out. It's so long, in fact, that the opening webpage tells you to block out your entire day to answer it.

Not to brag, but it only took me five hours…with a healthy hour's intermission to masturbate. The questions just got so specific. So visceral.

But I know myself.

I know what I've been craving for the last ten years. A single night when I was sixteen changed my entire understanding of pleasure and pain…and left me deeply unfulfilled. I've been trying to recapture that moment ever since, like a scab I can't quit picking.

Which is why I leapt at the chance to apply to The Company as soon as I learned of its existence. It's not the sort of place that advertises in the yellow pages or even with a mainstream searchable website. No, I had to learn about it from Lucy, a partner at my firm, who let it slip that she was a member one evening when after-work drinks became an all-night bender. I had to corner her in her office the next day until she told me more.

The Company, she said, fulfills fantasies. Not just run-of-the-mill plumber or cowboy or naughty boss scenarios, but intimate catered fantasies that bulldoze through all social manners and decorum to plumb the depths of your psyche, your past. What you *truly* desire.

"You won't want it, Ava," Lucy tried to warn me.

"Why not?"

I'd expected her to say because it was evil or insidious or run by criminals, but no, she simply said, "Because you'll never stop wanting it once you try it. Believe me, I gave into the temptation twenty years ago and they're the only ones who've been able to satisfy me since. What they're capable of…it warps your mind. Takes over everything. It's like an addiction. Everything I do now revolves around my next experience with them."

"That's not…" I couldn't really believe what she was saying, at least about herself. She's the senior partner at our law firm, one of—if not *the most*—decorated and venerated lawyers in our city. Respected. Admired. Definitely rational.

Also filthy rich. She would have to be, to afford twenty years of The Company's services. They don't come cheap.

But I just won a major case—the first big win of my career—and I'm rewarding myself with this.

It took three months to convince Lucy I truly wanted to be a member. Another month for them to process all my labs, computer, and questionnaire.

Then, one night I arrived home to find a letter propped against my condo door. A plain, thick cream envelope with my name written on it in elegant script sat on the stoop, fastened with a red wax seal of broken chain links wrapped around the words *concede voluptati—surrender to pleasure.*

I hadn't even turned on all the lights in my house before I locked the door and broke the seal. The small square of velvety stock paper inside smelled faintly of ocean brine and old wood, and I could have sworn the red ink glistened like fresh blood in the golden light.

> *Welcome to The Company, Ava St. Jude.*
> *Await further instructions and prepare.*

A curled finger of chill slid along my lowest ribs as I read it over and over and once the surprise melted away, I was left wet and hot and panting with anticipation.

It was finally happening.

My desire.

My darkest night revisited.

I only managed to convince Lucy to tell me about her experiences once, before she offered to nominate me if I kept her secret and stopped asking about it. And the fantasy she chose to share? It haunted my pleasure sessions for months, inserting myself into her scenario.

It was the specificity. The level of detail The Company had brought to life. I'd asked her how they knew and even she wasn't sure, but the effort they'd put into the scenario had left her not only awestruck but so impressed she returned to them again and again.

"The pleasure was absolute," she'd said. "Not just in my mind or body. It was like they hit bedrock and built from there. I came so many times I passed out in the end and woke up to a Company post-care employee measuring my vital signs."

"How long was it before you went back to them?"

"Seven days." Whatever my reaction, she added, "And that was only because that's how long it took me to dream up my next scenario."

"How long did it take them to fulfill it?"

"A month. The more specific the scenario, the more time they need to make it possible."

It had taken them seventy-six days to arrange mine. And every. single. day. I'd arrived home and held my breath as I walked up the steps to my condo, hoping I'd see a new envelope waiting for me.

I suppose mine had the added punishment element to arrange.

As well as the other people.

Mine doesn't just involve me.

Mine is as much about fixing a past wrong as it is getting my rocks off, but there should be plenty of that too.

I can only hope it's as overwhelming as that night was long ago. The thrill, the danger. The intensity.

It's the passion I crave most.

Don't get me wrong, I've had lovers since, but they only seem to embody two flavors—gentle and underwhelming or brutal and painful. I don't want either.

There's a look I want in their eye.

An obsessive fire.

Like I'm the only woman in the world who could ever satisfy them.

Like they'll die tomorrow if they don't taste me today.

I've arrived home tonight—day seventy-seven—to find a red box with a gold ribbon leaning against my door.

I stand in front of it for what feels like hours, holding my breath, letting the flutter of excitement ravage my heart. It's so strong the beat changes; I hardly recognize it.

Thunder rumbles heavily overhead. A massive "storm of

the century" is due to hit my city this weekend, only it's not exactly once a century; I experienced one ten years ago and it's one I'll never forget.

It must be the reason it took them so long to arrange my fantasy; they had to wait for a storm to come.

Lightning flashes, drawing my gaze behind me to the illuminated sky and the darkened street. My eye catches on a tiny flicker of orange. A cigarette cherry in a powder blue Cadillac parked halfway up the block.

There's a man sitting in it.

No, *men*.

I can't see their faces.

Can't tell their ages or heights or races.

Are they here for me?

They can't be. I specifically said no smokers—

My breath catches as I watch the Cadillac's window roll down. The cigarette soars out into the night like a tiny comet. A tan elbow lands on the open windowsill, then a muscled arm emerges and waves something at me—a nicotine gum packet—before the pieces of him retract and the window rolls up again.

So they're the actors The Company hired. I guess they're more than actors, though, aren't they.

Gigolos?

Escorts?

I'm frozen in place for a long beat studying their silhouettes, wondering how similar they'll be to the men from my past. There should be three, but I can only see the two up front. Maybe the last is in the back seat lying down? Or is he somewhere else?

Not in my house. Our experience hasn't started yet.

They shouldn't even know where I live technically. I was told they wouldn't be given that information.

But given the scenario I asked The Company for, maybe they took liberties to get the details right.

Although, there were plenty of details I never told them...

Checking my home security system just in case, I leave the shadows to it and scoop the box up, locking the door behind me before dashing to the kitchen for a bottle of wine, then to my plush red sofa. Better to savor its comfort and softness now knowing tomorrow won't bring me either of those things.

I steel myself with a stiff gulp before untying the ribbon and removing the box's top. The Company's message to me lies on top of other things, once again written on velvet stock paper, in bright red ink.

But my eyes catch on the objects underneath—an ornate black lace masquerade half-mask, the one I'll use to conceal my identity, as well as a bracelet of chain links. The bracelet is heavy and buzzes slightly against my skin, raising the goosebumps on my body like a kiss from a stranger.

I realize why the second I slip it on. The chains snap tight around my wrist, locking into place with an impossibly strong bond. There's no latch, but I try prying it off anyway. It doesn't give at all; if I got even slightly dehydrated it'd probably cut off circulation.

At least it's not painful.

The bracelet's actually sort of pretty...in a possessive, claiming way.

So is the letter, which is longer than the one I received before. Not by much, but enough that I flick on the end table lamp for an additional pool of light so I don't miss a thing.

A knot tangles at the back of my throat as I realize...they've sent me rules and warnings.

Your experience begins after nightfall tomorrow, so we've called in sick for you at your firm. Rest and prepare. Try not to resist and keep your wits about you. It will be everything you've dreamed of and more.

However.

Remember that this experience does not only involve you. You have until midnight tonight to back out. Do not put on the link bracelet until you've made your decision. Once the cancellation period has passed, your participation is mandatory.

Well, I guess it's a good thing I have no intention of backing out.

Also take heed of the rules:

1. *We have safety proofed this experience as much as is possible, but things happen, so remain vigilant throughout your catered experience. The Company is not responsible for mishaps.*
2. *Bring nothing extraneous with you—no phone, no keys, no wallet. You <u>will</u> be frisked and violations will be punished.*
3. *All members with knowledge of your fantasy will be wearing chain link bracelets for easy identification. Do not attempt to remove yours at any time.*
4. *Please refer to your gentlemen as Crimson, Sky, and Shadow. Per your request, they will call you 'Little Witch.' <u>REFRAIN from calling them baby, honey, or any other such endearment</u>. They have been carefully matched for you…but so have you for them. This is for your protection.*
5. *There are no safe words.*

I blink at the fourth rule, shivering with a little fear but more disappointment. I asked for passion. How can there be passion if I can't pretend they're more than what they are? I suppose it's a relief that I have names to call them at least… The fact that I'm about to relive the most intimate experience of my life with three total strangers is already strange enough.

Fuck, what if it's too intense? What if I can't handle it?

No.

I need to purge that shitty thought from my head.

I've asked for this. Ordered it specifically.

This is my night.

They've promised me a flawless experience; all I need to do is submit to it.

CHAPTER 2

TEN YEARS EARLIER

"You make it so hard to love you sometimes."
I push out a breath, trying to force the tension in my shoulders away from my ears. I have to remember...Mom's had a tough day. She only says things like this when she's exhausted. And when I accidentally burn the spaghetti sauce.
"Sorry Mom."
"Don't be sorry. Be better."
I was trying to finish my Algebra II homework and forgot about the pan on the stove. I didn't mean to, but I've realized that "didn't mean to" isn't a good enough excuse. It doesn't make up for anything.
Mom avoids me as she comes around the table. Sucking my stomach in, I press to the wood so she can get by without having to touch me. But I'm too big and it's not enough space. As she shoves past, the clasp on her bag scrapes my back. I try not to gasp, but she hears it anyway and responds with a sound at the back of her throat I've heard too many times before.
"Wash your damned hair, Ava. I can practically see my reflection in it."
"Yes, ma'am."
"Do it now. I need you out of the house by nine."
I blink in confusion, digesting the words. Why would I need to—
"What did I just say? Go."

She doesn't yell—she never yells, never has to when her obsidian blade of a tongue slices deep with the softest whisper. I flinch anyway and dash for the hall, hoping I can outrun what I already know is coming. I don't make it in time.

I hear her yank the pan off the heat, murmuring, "Fat, useless piece of shit."

The rest of her words are cut off by a rumble of thunder and an echoing crack of lightning. It's been raining cats and dogs for hours.

Sharp pressure tightens in my chest as I duck into the bathroom and jump into the tub to wash. It's a quick rinse, a little floral shampoo I bought myself, and a brainstorm. I don't know where she wants me to go. It's Friday night in a town with more spare time than imagination. The over-21's are at the bars, and the under-21's are either at the movies or partying at the Stackman House until the break of dawn.

I don't have money for a movie—it was my week to cover groceries—which leaves the hell of other people.

But I...don't want to go to that house. The Stackman mansion is not a place for people like me. Nerdy losers with no real friends just trying to survive to their eighteenth birthday so they can escape aren't welcome there.

Tonight especially, I don't want to go. The popular kids are doing some weird mystery blowout, all decked out and masked and humping each other like it's their last day on Earth.

Or so I've heard.

It's supposed to be insane. Mayhem. Our town sits at the center of a cluster of others that all share a single massive high school, and it's massive because there's nothing to do out here in the boonies but bone more townies into existence.

All those kids. All those swirling hormones.

But at least they'll all be masked tonight. And the house will be dry. Maybe I can find a room and hole up in it until the storm breaks. Then I can come home and sneak in through the window or something.

I don't have much to wear, but I find an old witch's hat at the back of my closet, a black dress I've had since I was ten that used to reach my calves but now ends just above my knees and which strangles my tits into an embarrassing pushed-up position near my throat. Then I throw on a black dollar store mask that covers my eyes. I already know my tennis shoes—my only closed-toed shoes—will flood as soon as I get outside, but there's not much I can do about that. I throw the getup on and grab my keys-wallet-umbrella with seconds to spare before there's a harsh bang on my bedroom door.

"You gone yet?"

I jerk the door open with my hands already raised. "I'm going."

She eyes my costume as if she expected better with the five minutes she gave me. "Why do you do this to yourself?"

I don't really know what to say to that. When she's in moods like this, she's more t-rex than human. I've learned to stand still until she loses interest and moves on with an eyeroll.

I'm down the stairs and out the door five seconds later; anywhere is better than being trapped in a house with her.

CHAPTER 3

I'm washed, plucked, and waxed to within an inch of my life by the time six p.m. rolls around and there's a knock at my door. A delivery person wearing a chain-link bracelet hands me a garment bag and leaves without saying a single word. Inside, I find my outfit for the evening. My costume. The one I suggested to The Company when they told me their theme for tonight—a masquerade ball. It's a ball gown fit for French royalty, except it's lighter, thinner, so I can run in it when the time comes. For that, they've provided a pair of black waterproof jogging shoes that are just fancy enough to look like they match. I already know they're going to hurt anyway, since I haven't had the chance to break them in, but sometimes fantasies hurt. This one definitely will. And I'm prepared anyway. Ever since that first warning from The Company to prepare, I've been running sprints at the gym; I can last for a solid half mile now before I get winded.

With the lace mask they provided, I don't recognize myself, which is the point. This is who I wished I could have been ten years ago, when the worst people did the worst things to me.

Gah, I'm ashamed that after all this time, even thinking about thinking about what they did to me makes me want to curl into a ball and die a little. I've worked so hard to get over it but ten years on, my tormentors' laughter still rings in my ears.

It took years of therapy to realize I never deserved what they did to me. They hurt me because they could, they wanted to. My therapist tried to help me understand that they were acting out their own disfunctions on me, but honestly that didn't make any of it better.

It didn't make the trauma easier to bear either.

In fact, it made tonight an inevitability.

As I make an early dinner for myself in the kitchen, dancing around to my favorite epic girl bops, I know no amount of therapy will ever pull the same healing weight as what I get to do tonight.

No matter what my therapist says, sometimes forgiveness hurts more than it helps.

Sometimes time doesn't heal; it only festers.

I try to eat the butter garlic pasta I made with some sense of civility, but it's not possible. Not with my jitters. So I eat it over the sink like a goblin.

I'm halfway through the plate when a text comes in on my phone.

Your thighs look delicious tonight.

It's from an unmarked number.

My eyes dart for the windows that line the back wall of my condo. The backyard is empty, quiet, and completely pitch black.

I wish I could lick that little bit of sauce off your lip.

It's like I can't stop myself; my tongue flicks out to clean my mouth and there's instantly a response.

Slower.

A buzz warms my center. This never happened that night ten years ago, but so far, it's a welcome addition and improvement.

Dragging my attention back to the wall of windows, I study the darkness, wondering where he is. Who he is.

My curiosity gets the better of me as I text back, *Is this Crimson, Sky, or Shadow?*

:) Guess. I'll give you a reward if you're right.
Give me a clue.
I taste like metal and drip like wine.
Blood. Blood is...
Crimson?
You're just full of surprises.

I stare at the message. My face twists with uncertainty and my heart spasms with panic.

Those words...

Those *exact* words...

They're a detail from that night The Company shouldn't know.

Couldn't know because I never told them.

I force a jagged breath out and slap my cheek until I stop overthinking.

This has always been my problem. My superpower, but also my problem. I don't trust easily. Why would I? My job as a criminal defense attorney gives me backstage access to the horrible things people do to one another every day.

Crimson's messages *must* be part of the experience. It would be insane timing if some rando was texting me like this, tonight of all nights. It must be part of the storytelling, laying the groundwork for my scenario. They did thorough research so Crimson could pretend to be one of my tempter-tormentors from the past.

Which means I don't need to freak out. I need to yield or I'll ruin my own damned fantasy before it even begins.

Tonight is history re-envisioned.

Tonight is fiction.

The curtain is rising. The stage is set. The play is finally—

Knock-knock-knock. The quick raps on the door bring me crashing back into the present moment. Defying every survival instinct I've honed over a quarter-lifetime of suffering, I lay the phone aside gently and step away. Ten paces bring me to the door. The camera panel on the wall shows me there are two masked men waiting patiently outside—one wears a red mask, the other a black one. Both hold their arms up toward the camera so I can see the chain link bracelets around their wrists.

Crimson and Shadow.

They look like harbingers of doom.

They look like angels of vengeance.

They look like everything I've been dreaming of.

CHAPTER 4

TEN YEARS EARLIER

The bass beat rattles the foundations of the earth. I can feel it in the stairs beneath my feet and the hairs along my arms. Little puddles to either side of the Stackman House's front walk quiver with rhythmic ripples.

No one's outside, not in this weather.

Not with the blackened sky roaring and raging like this.

It took me twenty minutes to run here and I'm soaked and shivering by the time I push the mansion's door open. It's both warped with dry rot and now entirely saturated with storm, so it moves like a rotten wall, slamming inward with a groan, hitting the wall and all but announcing my arrival.

Not that anybody cares. More people than I've ever seen in my life crowd every corner of the foyer and the rooms beyond. So many kids stand on the warped and buckling grand staircase, I only know there are holes in it by the gaps between people.

"Door! Door! Door!" They chant like they've been doing it all night.

I reach for the edge but there's already a hand under mine. Warm. Larger. It's their size that makes me pull my own hand away.

"Sorry!"

My eyes snap upward and I think I should recoil harder. Farther. The hand belongs to a boy. A guy. Tall and possibly carved from stone with a pronounced Adam's apple and...red eyes. Red Halloween novelty contacts. They're not part of the mask he's wearing. It's some horror character I'm not familiar with, but his buddy beside him is wearing the same one so it must be popular. The only difference between their outfits is that Red-Eyes' mask is splattered with blood, and his buddy with eyes so dark they're black wears a burned mask.

My gaze darts away from both.

I find an empty spot on the door edge and heave while they push. Together, we fight against the howling wind to shut the entry tight. With the door closed, it's like the storm barely exists at all, fading to nothing but atmosphere as the golden glow from the chandelier overhead flickers. Warmth from somewhere beats back the cold. Despite how chilled and sopping I am in my wet clothes, it doesn't seem like the worst place to spend the night.

I feel something against my back and turn to find Red-Eyes staring down at me. Black-Eyes is there, too, a couple feet away.

"Oh, sorry, thank you!" I try to shout over the music. "For helping with the...door."

Red-Eyes cocks his head a little.

"I know you." His voice catches me off-guard. It's familiar. Deep and gentle, but hollowed by the space inside the mask.

My hand instinctively rises to check that my mask is still in place...but so does his.

I freeze as his hand sweeps up to press gently at the edges of the plastic against my cheek, not to take my mask off but to make sure I don't. The warm graze of his fingertips shocks my system. It's been so long since I've felt someone else's touch, it burns. Scalds. I yank my head away before I risk getting used to it, ducking my chin, hoping they'll be gone when I look up again.

But they don't go. Gaze on the floor, I watch their feet

take a step closer and my stomach sinks with apprehension.

I shouldn't have come. I made it all of three feet in the door before I was in over my head.

I don't know this stuff. What I'm supposed to do.

All I know is that whoever they are, they found me too fast to have good intentions.

They're sharks circling.

I should leave and find an all-night diner. Maybe a bus station. Maybe just pick a bus once I get there and never come back.

But the storm laughs at the thoughts in my head; the next clap of thunder is so loud it nearly drowns out the music, all but warning me that I'm not going anywhere any time soon.

And the guys are still there, leering when I look up.

"Why don't you dress like this normally?" Red-Eyes asks, his heated gaze skating across my lips-chin-neck-chest.

Before he can sear my bare legs, I try to tuck them away.

"It's just something I threw together," I respond.

He nods at his friend as if I've said something profound. Then we linger there, staring at each other for a private eternity, until I come to my senses.

"Well...bye."

I turn and bolt for another room where I think I can see the glow from a fire. I need some space. I need a drink. And I need to forget what the warmth of his fingers feels like before I do something incredibly stupid.

CHAPTER 5

A deep inhale is all I allow myself before I yank open my front door and come face to face with my dark escorts for the evening. My nostrils flood with that stormy electrical charge scent, rain on asphalt and soil, and nothing else.

No cologne.

No lotion.

Relief floods my system, cooling engines I never realized were overheating.

They listened. I specifically requested my men be clean and washed, but not to use anything scented on their skin. It was such an important detail…and The Company listened.

That alone is almost worth the small mortgage I paid for tonight.

I don't realize I'm smiling until Crimson's hand rises to my cheek. His thumb traces the curve of my smile and the edges of his lips tip up in return, summoning a shiver I can feel all the way to my tailbone.

Their masks only cover their brows, eyes, and cheekbones, leaving the rest of them open to adoration, and there's plenty to adore. Crimson's red matte mask is faceted like a ruby, but still molded to his high cheekbones, around his almond eyes, with a crimson ribbon tied in his dark tousled hair. His jaw is gorgeously angular, not overly square, not rounded, just…distinguished. His full lips have a cupid's bow…just like Red-Eyes had all those years ago. I smile again at the attention to detail. The man beside him wears a faceted mask in clouded black, like smoky quartz. His lips are wider, a tiny bit thinner and his chin has a dimple in it. His dirty blond hair is unexpected, but washed and combed. So are the tattoos peeking out of the collar and cuffs of his suit. Yet they found someone with pitch black eyes just like the boy from long ago. This must be…

"Shadow?"

He nods, no hint of a smile on his face.

"And you're Crimson?" I ask to include the one who's still cradling my cheek.

He nods. That dark grin slides higher up one side of his face, like he's…relieved.

I don't have the courage to ask about what.

But there's something about the combination of his relieved smile and the unwavering focus in his gaze that tightens a dark knot low in my belly.

Their costumes are vastly different from that night long ago—embellished dark suits that fit their physiques to perfection at my request and look a little like what a vampire might wear a couple hundred years ago—but the effect of the pair of them is spot on. Standing there, staring through my soul as the rain pours down behind them, they invoke the exact shade of déjà vu I'd been hoping for. My core flutters with anticipation.

Crimson nods to Shadow who pops open a massive umbrella before Crimson offers me his hand.

It's time, his gaze tells me.

But there's an "incorrect" detail here that nips at me, even though I don't want it to.

The boy ten years ago had red eyes. Sure; they were fake slasher red—costume red contacts—but they've haunted me through the years like glimpses of a boogeyman only seen in shadow underneath the bed.

These eyes. Crimson's eyes. They consume me in a

different way.

They're three different colors. The outer edges are green as summer grass running into a brown so light it looks orange until it collides with gold near the irises. Like some sort of melting sherbert.

He clocks my hesitation...and smirks.

"Not bloody enough for you?"

My body reacts viscerally to his voice, which...is modulated. I don't know how, there are no bulges in odd places to suggest a sound pack, but it's deep and low and slightly artificial. It sounds like the purr of an engine.

I swallow, eyes darting toward Shadow, wondering if he sounds the same even though I never heard him speak, not even back then, before settling my gaze on Crimson again.

It's not that I don't like his eyes—they're gorgeous, whoever he is, he has the genetics of a god—but will he be able to scare me the way my bloody-faced tempter once did?

He seems to read my thoughts. "Don't worry. You'll fear me long before the night is through."

He offers me his hand again and I take it. The pads of my soft paper-pushing fingertips caress the callouses on his. It's strange to think of a male escort having callouses at all, even if his work *is* manual labor in a manner of speaking. Maybe he has a hobby.

I snort, realizing what it must be—woodworking. Any escort good enough for The Company would definitely know how to work his wood.

But the joy of the pun dies pretty immediately, replaced by frost and fear.

I'm meant to sleep with these men tonight. These dark strangers.

And not just sleep. Fuck their brains out. Or have mine fucked out? Either way, it's part of the fantasy, the one I spent hours laying out on paper, visualizing every detail of what I wanted, how I wanted it. It had turned me on like nothing else, knowing that I could demand anything. Knowing real men were on standby to give me exactly what I want.

Most people fantasize with no expectation that their secret desires will ever come true. When faced with an offer to make it happen, would they want to? Could they handle it? Would they chicken out?

There is no backing out now. Tonight is a freedive into the ocean. I'm already pulling strokes deeper into the darkness and even if I wanted to pull out now I couldn't; I have to reach the surface again before I can take a breath.

Crimson opens the back door to the powder blue Cadillac for me and slides in after, sealing us in. A second later, Shadow rounds the car and jumps in the driver's seat. His dark gaze connects with mine in the rearview mirror before darting sideways to Crimson. Something unspoken passes between them, but I don't know if I'm supposed to ask. So I stay quiet until long after we pull away from the curb.

Rain whips at the car in white sheets, making it almost impossible to see out. But it's the winds that rock the car on the road; they keep the energy inside knotted and high. Shadow's massive hands are tight on the wheel, making adjustments as needed, but there's tension in his shoulders and neck. Like he's afraid of the storm and trying to hide it.

I have the strangest desire to—

It's only when you're free to do anything that you realize how often you hold yourself back. Under normal circumstances, I'd never dream of running my fingers through the hair of a stranger driving me to an undisclosed destination, but these aren't normal circumstances. And I want a different sort of tension tonight.

A quick click and my seatbelt slides away across my chest, drawing Crimson's narrowed gaze. He watches me slide closer, into the middle. Watches me reach forward and sweep my fingers into the thick wheatish hair at the back of

Shadow's head.

Shadow stiffens further, but I'm almost certain it's just surprise. Still, I say, "It's okay. I won't hurt you. I'm scared of storms too."

Gently. Slowly. I run my fingers along his scalp, then down over the tattooed skin of his neck. They're clouds...his tattoos, I mean. Delicate exaggerated clouds like you might see in a painting, outlined in black but shaded with mauve—storm clouds.

It occurs to me that they might be fake, a bit of evocative costuming. After all, these guys would have read my application, my writing of that night, to help with their characters. They would know everything that happened to me happened during a "storm of the century..."

Discomfort skitters down my spine. There are certain things you forget, basic things. Like the fact that I opened up my most private moments to be turned into a sort of erotic stage play involving other people. People who would have had to read my file, read my recollections, my fears and insecurities, my darkest needs, to actually play their parts. These two actors—and whoever's waiting for us at our "theater"—probably know more about me now than my therapist does.

The problem with that is that I've never told *anybody* the full story of that night. Not my friends, not past boyfriends. What my therapist knows is a bland summary in contrast to what I told The Company.

I poured my heart out in that application because I wanted this so badly.

And now I'm caressing the head of some rando who's read my private diary so he can pretend to be obsessed with me.

Embarrassment isn't the right word for it.

I'm just self-conscious. I don't think it's anything to be ashamed of. I've paid for this—I can do whatever I want tonight—but it's new and I've never liked being vulnera—

Something tugs at my abdomen, pulling me back into the present moment. Shadow's gaze darts from the road to mine in the mirror again and again as I realize I've stopped petting him. My hand is just cradling his neck now. Crimson's taut arm is around my waist when I hear a *click*. His arm pulls forward and I slide backward, away from Shadow, against the seatback as Crimson tightens the middle seatbelt against my hips.

His sherbert eyes are only inches from mine, locked on me in a way that makes me think he's envious of the attention I was paying Shadow. His hand creeps onto my stomach and rests there, drawing soft circles around my bellybutton with his thumb.

"Shadow's not afraid of storms," he says after a moment. "He wants you to enjoy tonight. He wants you to trust us."

I could lie and say I do, but something about the way he looks at me makes me want to tell him the truth. "I don't know how."

The car swerves and I glance away long enough to realize we're in the middle of nowhere—a forest, I think?—and Shadow has guided us into a paved pull off under some trees. We're protected enough that the sound of rain patter dulls to a deep sigh rather than battering the roof like ammunition.

"Why are we stopping?"

Shadow doesn't answer. He puts the car in park but leaves it on. Another second and he launches himself out into the weather, shuts the door, then opens mine and climbs in beside me, moist and panting. The door shuts us in again, swaddling us in silence.

A silence so hot my skin feels like it's burning.

There's no space back here.

Especially not when Crimson cinches the belt around me an inch tighter, securing me in place. I can't help it. My gaze volleys between them in fascination.

"We were told to wait," is all Crimson says, like he's admonishing himself for what he's already decided they're going to do.

Shadow hasn't even settled in the seat yet when his hand curves around my chin and pulls my face toward him. For a moment, I think he's going to kiss me. Or speak; he seems to have something he desperately wants to say to me. But he runs his piercing dark gaze across my features before he turns my head slightly away and plunges for my neck instead.

His pillowy lips.

His hungry teeth.

A nip.

A lick of his tongue.

A gasp escapes me like a sigh, and Shadow makes the first sound he's made since we met—an echo of the same only deeper. It spurs him on. He tines his fingers into my hair and fists them, holding my head still as he bites my neck again, so hard I wonder for a second if he's going to draw blood.

Even if he does—I yelp with pleasure. The tickle and wriggling surprise of it, it's like sparks under the skin. I'm already wetter than I've been in months. Years.

I want to turn toward him, seize his lips with mine, but he won't let me. When I try, Shadow tugs tighter at my hair and moves down to kiss and caress my shoulder as Crimson wraps his hand around my throat.

My eyes go wide. It's pure instinct to claw at his wrist and try to pull it away. It doesn't matter anymore that my mind knows it's make believe. My body knows he's going to hurt me.

"Easy." His whisper could command armies. "This is for you. This is all for you."

It's not easy at all.

"Hands on your tits," he says, tightening his grasp on my

throat in increments that have me panting instead of suffocating. "Now, little witch."

His fingers tighten again and my hands palm my breasts, my nipples like diamond through the fabric. Clutching them is the only way to keep my hands distracted from trying to escape.

"That's our girl," he purrs. "Now relax or you'll ruin our fun."

Only when I force myself to untense does his grip loosen. He rewards me with a kiss to my cheek, a tiny flickering lick to my jaw. His breath wafts into my nose when he pecks the corner of my lips, filling me with the scent of peppermint. It's warm and inviting and...so wholesome in contrast to the moment, I can't help but study his face when he pulls back.

The dark confidence is still there, but it's mixed with something that shoots right for my thighs, slamming them together with need.

Shadow catches my ear between his teeth, drawing my gaze to him. The look on his face? Fixation. Curiosity. Warning.

To their unspoken question I nod, because that's all I can do. Their hands—on my throat and in my hair—twitch with frenzied anticipation.

Crimson presses something hard to my lips—his thick middle and forefinger slip past and pry my teeth apart before spearing my mouth deep. I fight the urge to gag as he pushes them against my tongue again and again, petting it like he's trying to read braille. Then he withdraws slowly, watching the string of saliva that trails between them and my lips like he wants to lick it off but is trying to resist.

Shadow's long, strong fingers replace Crimson's before I can breathe, and this time they dive so deep down my throat I can't help but gag. I reach to pull him out—

Crimson catches my arm.

Then his mouth is there against my ear and... "Hands on

your tits, or you'll be running with handcuffs on tonight."

There's no malice in his voice. Only excitement, like he owns both paths before me and is only intrigued to see which I'll choose. Shadow's fingers are still in my mouth, massaging my tongue, when I force my hands back to my breasts. He makes that breathy grunt again and pushes his fingers even deeper. I cough, sputter, but he seems to think I'm serenading him. His head falls against mine as he listens; his heartbeat revs with every sound he forces out of me. And when a tear reaches the corner of my eye, he studies it like a precious thing.

Stares.

Considers.

His eyes, I realize, aren't actually black; they're the singed gray of arson. But it hardly matters. The tear finally slips from my eye and the tip of his tongue catches it before it can touch the mask, collects it, ferries it back to his mouth to taste.

The moment catches me completely off guard. It's predatory. It's invasive. It's intense and strangely erotic and almost what I asked for, except twisted. I have no idea why they would think this is part of our script. Unless they got the wrong one?

Yet I can't deny that the sight of his tongue, the slick warmth of that flickering lick, has me aching for him to do it again. To summon another tear to drink. Or sup from the moisture in my mouth, my—

"I know what she needs," Crimson croons.

I tear my gaze from Shadow's conquest to see Crimson has pulled my knees apart and draped one over his thigh. Shadow mirrors him on my other side, spreading me wide and open between them.

Too wide. Too open.

The tiny strip of fabric pretending to be underwear barely covers anything.

I automatically try to close my legs—

"Uh-uh. You'll miss the show."

Shadow pushes my head forward, away from the seat, so I have a full view of myself on display. Crimson's fingers slide slowly down my inner thigh, taking their time. A little swirl here, a little squeeze there. All the while, their tiny sounds of hunger and need serenade me. My pussy quivers with an impatience I can taste on my tongue.

Crimson reaches the waistband of my underwear. He runs a single finger along the edge like it's some forcefield holding him back…until Shadow suddenly growls from my other side. His broad hand dives for the thinnest part of the fabric, sweeps between it and my skin and twists it around his fist. There's a moment of tension, a pinch of pain, and then the fabric is flying as Shadow tosses the tattered remnants of my underwear into the front somewhere.

Neither pays attention to where they land; the only thing they care about is my pussy. They seem fixated on it. Mesmerized. Crimson and Shadow each slide a hand into place along my high inner thigh to either side and squeeze, teasing at my soft pink lips with the very edge of their fingers.

"Beautiful," Crimson murmurs. "Don't you agree, Shadow?"

"Perfect."

Shadow's voice is also modulated, but it's slightly rasped and smoky. When was the last time he spoke? Is he really such a man of few words that this is a special moment?

No. It must just be part of the play.

"Little witch, what do you think?"

Huh?

When I realize he's actually asking me, all I want to do is close my legs again, but they tighten their hold on my thighs and Shadow nudges my head that much farther forward.

"Aren't you perfect?"

But the words won't come. They lodge behind my teeth, refusing to budge. The touches, the caresses, *they've* been close to perfect. I don't want to ruin it by lying about my perfection. Bile rises in me at the thought of voicing those words; they're a joke and exactly what I don't want to hear tonight—not at my expense, at least.

Crimson's technicolor gaze snaps to me almost in anger. "Don't you think you're perfect?"

"I-It's fine," I say, just wanting this moment to end.

But it doesn't. It happens so fast I only register the sudden bite of pain after Crimson's hand slaps my pussy. I cry out in shock more than anything, but he strangles the cry, his hand back around my throat, not choking, just holding. He pulls me against him, his nose pressed to my cheek.

His voice grinds out, "You think you can say that about our girl and get away with it? Huh?"

Slap. Slap! SLAP!

This second swell from Shadow is harder but somehow less painful. Maybe because they hit my lips more than my clit, but *damn.*

"What the hell!" I shout.

It's no use. Shadow's fingers are there, massaging softly, gently, a second later. Soothing away the hurt. He teases my clit, circles it, rubs with soft featherlike caresses, before the pad of his finger connects and slides past it to pet the slit beyond, and dip deeper. He smiles at the wetness already there, baring his straight white teeth in a cheshire grin that terrifies me.

He parts my lips just long enough to plunge the two fingers he shoved down my throat inside as deep as they will go, filling me.

"Fuck me!" I cry out in surprise.

Crimson's deep modulated giggle dances across my skin. "In time."

Shadow nibbles my neck again while his fingers dive in

and out until we can hear the sucking wetness as my pussy clings to him, trying to keep him inside. Then he crooks his fingers, finds that spot inside, and TV static fills my vision. Ecstasy spreads like watercolor in hues I've never seen before.

"You need me, too, you know," Crimson whispers. His fingertip lands on my bud and strokes in time with Shadow.

The sight of their hands working in tandem against me—for my pleasure—it's like Greek fire. I now know *exactly* what Lucy was talking about. This night has already delivered the vibe of that evening ten years ago and the main event hasn't even happened yet; I'm in for an experience I already know I'll want to repeat as soon as possible.

All my planning, all my fantasizing, pales in comparison to this.

When Crimson's caress of my clit halts, I can't help but cry with desperation and frustration, both of which only exaggerate the pulsing throbbing bliss of Shadow's continued strokes deep inside me.

Crimson smiles at my despair. Fuck, he's teasing me. But only for a moment before he shifts the two fingers he had in my mouth to my entrance. Shadow's fingers push lower toward the back of the channel. His grip on my hair tightens so I can't glance away as Crimson drives his fingers in alongside Shadow's.

I thought I was full before.

I thought two was pushing it.

But suddenly there are four and I feel stretched to madness. They piston their fingers in and up alongside one another in a hummingbird-fast rhythm that blinds me. What did Lucy call it? Absolute pleasure?

Mind-blowing doesn't come close. Mind-erasing, maybe.

I can't breathe, can't do anything but succumb to the brutal onslaught.

And then Crimson's thumb creeps up to my clit, rubbing-

rubbing, and my eyes roll back. It's like the storm is inside me, thunder rumbles, lightning flashes, and my body bucks against the seatbelt pinning me down until I know I'll bruise tomorrow. If there is a tomorrow. My heart isn't racing, it's overheating like some sort of enigma machine with a spanner in the works.

The orgasm seizes control of me, arrests my muscles. All I can feel is their hands on my thighs, the thrust of their fingers unrelenting, and their kisses against either side of my neck.

It isn't one wave but many ripples growing and growing until the tide pulls back and crashes through my body as they just keep stroking, drawing it out. One builds the foundation for the next and my expectations wash away with the rising and sinking tides.

Then whiteness comes. Mindlessness takes me. Paradise is born.

Faintly through the roar in my ears, I hear Crimson say, "See? Perfect."

And darkness pulls me under.

CHAPTER 6

TEN YEARS EARLIER

Sometimes I feel so invisible I could scream. It comes with the territory when you're the town pariah. My family's poor. My father abandoned us. My mom has a "reputation." I wear clothes from the secondhand consignment store. It doesn't matter that I have the highest grades in my year; as far as everyone in my town is concerned I was marked for failure from the get-go. In movies and tv, that sort of origin story inspires sympathy. In real life, people think that means they can treat you like shit.

Maybe invisibility is safer than the alternative, though.

There must be at least four hundred people in this dilapidated old house. I've chosen a quiet spot where I can observe everybody in peace, but I envy the little cliques I can see from here. A group sits on the couches by the fire. Little trios and quads half-dance, bob, and weave with red solo cups in hand. A couple tables are set up for beer pong along the far wall and a whole mass of people are over by the heap of beer kegs and bottles that they've piled on the sheet-covered furniture to the side.

But everyone's in costumes tonight. Frankenstein's putting a fairy on his shoulders. A ghost with four legs and two heads is groping itself against a far wall. And there are so many black cats and "dead" football players I can tell nobody really cares about the costumes, only the anonymity their personas offer.

Maybe I should've stayed and talked with those two guys by the door.

I don't know if I'm ever going to get the normal high school experience, but nobody's voluntarily giving it to me.

I catch sight of myself in a mirror and I'm convinced the blood-splattered guy was lying when he said he knew who I was. The mask is cheap but it covers enough features that I just look like the other witches here, ignoring the slight rattiness of my clothes. I stood by the fire drying my dress for like 20 minutes. It made the fabric wrinkle and bunch, but it kinda adds to the vibe rather than detracting.

Bravery's the problem. I've never had much of it, except where Big Picture stuff is concerned. I've been counting down the days until I turn 18—literally, I have a calendar under my mattress and I X out every 24-hour period between me and my freedom like they're grains of sand in an hourglass. I know when the day comes, I'm out of here; it's why I have two after-school jobs—one that pays my part of the expenses my mom asks for each month and one she doesn't know about. I squirrel that money away under the floorboards and I have enough for the deposit and first three months on my own apartment in the city. By the time I'm actually eighteen, I'll have enough to invest in a money market account. I've been studying up on it during my lunch break at school, using the library computers.

I think that would surprise literally everyone in this town, to know I have that sort of scratch. But I like having a secret. I like knowing that the only thing holding me back is time. Not even that much, just thirteen months, then I'm finally free.

"Hey witch, do you play?"

I blink away my daydreams to find a guy in a mask near the beer pong table staring at me. It's the same mask that a quarter of the guys here seem to be wearing—the same one the two by the front door had. Except his is spraypainted blue with a star on one cheek and the number 74 on the other. I think it's some sort of sports thing.

"Me?" I ask just to be sure.

"Yeah," he laughs. "We need another player. You in?"

I've never played before, but I should. I'm here anyway. And when am I going to get another chance to be like everybody else?

"I'll have to watch you do it first," I tell him as I approach.

"Don't worry, you're with me, I got you," he says, tossing a welcoming arm around my shoulder, smothering me in the scent of his cologne—sage and lemon and orange. His touch and his smell are so unexpected, so inviting, I already feel myself wishing he'd keep his arm around me. It sucks wishing this was my every day. Instead, it feels like An Event, something rare.

"Hey, who wants to play us?" Blue-Mask yells.

A few heads turn our direction, but no one comes forward until two familiar "faces" walk into view at the other end of the table. Red-Eyes and Black-Eyes stare me down across the way. Despite their entire faces being obscured by the masks, as Red-Eyes turns toward his friend, I get the distinct impression it's me they came to the table for, not the game. Is that right? It can't be. I have no idea who they are.

"Babe, who is this?"

I nearly jump out of my skin as someone arrives behind me, but I don't feel any better when I turn around and realize I know who she is. Emily Deutch. Cross a mean girl with a rabid chihuahua and put her in a princess dress, then send her out to commit war atrocities, and you might come close. She's the sort of popular girl who uses her power for evil intentionally, giving half the school PTSD in the process. She gets away with it because her mother is the high school principal, her dad's the local sheriff, and her hot older brother got a record deal and now opens for TayTay with his band Open-Heart Burglary—it's like a trifecta of fear and influence that keeps her popular no matter what she does. I know of at least half a dozen kids who've transferred schools just to get away from her.

"Hey, I didn't know if you were going to show," Blue-Mask says, wrapping his arms around her.

My stomach tightens as I realize he must be her boyfriend, Blake Sturgess. I just had Blake Sturgess's arm around my shoulder.

"Had to pick up Mike on the way." She motions to the behemoth behind her, a lumbering giant who I think plays for the basketball team. He's dressed head to toe in camo, going for some sort of action hero look, which only makes him seem like more of a swampy frat boy. "Who's your friend?"

"I needed a second," Blake says.

I take a step back. "It's fine. I don't need to play."

"No, stay," she commands, her voice dripping with boredom. "Play with those guys so it's three on three."

She motions to Red-Eyes and Black-Eyes, but there's no way to tell through the masks what they think of all this. I approach with caution, fully prepared to let them take all the shots and just leave me standing there.

Instead, they watch my every step to their side of the table like creepy moving statues, their heads turning slowly in unison to follow me.

"Hi again," I try. "You guys can play, I can just be here." They don't say anything for long enough, I think to add, "Or I can get out of here?"

"Bitch, I said play," Emily barks, drawing attention like a siren.

The music's loud enough to drown most of her voice out, but the radius of people around us hear it loud and clear.

The guys step to either side of me, sandwiching me between them, as Black-Eyes holds up the ball for me to go *first.*

"I don't know how," I admit, and he nods solemnly.

Red-Eyes slides a hand onto my shoulder. Even though I can't see his mouth, I can hear the dark smile in his voice as he purrs, "I bet you don't know how to do a lot of things. We can fix that."

CHAPTER 7

I've never passed out from pleasure before, but if it leaves me this relaxed, this unburdened of insecurities about the night to come, I won't be complaining any time soon.

I wake in motion, my head resting on Crimson's thigh, one of his hands keeping my mask from falling off while his other fingers trace an eerily gentle path through my hair. Shadow is driving again and when I sit up, he wears a smile as soft as Crimson's touch. But there isn't a matching smile on Crimson; he seems...bothered?

Is that right?

Something seems to have happened in however long I've been unconscious. They seem to have switched places emotionally.

"There she is," Shadow says, his voice pleased and relaxed even with the modulation. He meets my gaze in the rearview mirror like our world-shifting encounter in the back of this car completely shattered his shell from earlier.

"We're almost there," Crimson grumbles.

He won't meet my eye when I study him, and even though I can't see his eyebrows because of the mask, I can see the central creases on his forehead that suggest he's pensive, consumed by thought. His body language is stiff too.

But it's not my place to ask him if he's okay, is it? And I certainly don't want to ask him if he enjoyed doing that to me; do you ask escorts that sort of thing? I've never used one before so…

I definitely don't want to know if he *didn't* enjoy it. It would ruin the rest of the night.

It's not even my place to fluff up his ego, even though I could without telling a lie—that was the single most intense sexual experience of my life, and the fact that there should be more like it tonight, that I get to have them both again makes my mouth water and my pelvic floor contract eagerly.

Shadow, at least, grins flirtatiously at me, like he can read my mind.

I let myself smile back before turning to gaze out the window. We've entered a neighborhood I know relatively well where white-collar crime is simply a rite of admission. It's the sort of area where the roads are crowded by massive brick and stucco and wrought-iron fences guarding mansions so far back in the trees you can barely see their lights from the street.

Or maybe you can when the weather isn't like this. The rain is navigable, but only by the insane and vindictive. I don't hear any thunder but lightning dances across the narrow strip of visible sky overhead almost constantly. When Shadow pulls into a dark driveway a few moments later and rolls down the window to show the guy at the gatehouse his chain-link bracelet, the heavy, moist air promises the storm is far from over.

It also promises…roses; the air is heavy with their scent. The gate opens onto a garden of them, stretching the entire length and width of the lawn. But it's unlike any rose garden I've ever seen because the blooms glow neon in the darkness. Pink. White. Red. The flowers are so bright in comparison to their dark foliage they look like they're floating.

"What is this place?" It's a far cry from the decrepit old Stackman House.

The car pulls up to a valet station by the front walk and

both of my dark strangers exit the car and come around to open my door. Crimson takes door duty with the massive umbrella and Shadow offers me his arm.

Whatever brief malaise stole Crimson from me, I'm more relieved than I can say a moment later when Crimson offers me his arm too and he smiles at me.

United, they guide me toward the giant American gothic mansion up ahead. The motif of the glowing roses continues along the house's perimeter and around the sides, out of sight. Music booms through the windows, different from the hip hop of a decade ago but still basically the same. Modernized, energetic, foreboding.

"Ready?" Shadow asks after a moment.

I nod to let him know I am, but I also say, "It's different from what I imagined."

Different, but wonderful. Even though the music, the location, and the people are different, the atmosphere is unnervingly on point. So imposing, I feel like a lost, lonely teenager again, counting down the days until everything would finally be okay.

But were they? Ever? It's ten years later and the trauma's still slaughterhouse fresh.

They must be able to feel me tense through their grip on my arms, because my men crowd closer, almost consoling.

"The main events tonight will be the same," Crimson says. "But to maintain your anonymity, the aesthetic has been changed."

That makes sense, of course. I want revenge and to walk away with my life intact, so it's not like they could recreate that high school costume party to a tee. But what they have conjured up instead is above and beyond what I could hope for. I was picturing a prom strung together with bulk decorations and bake sale donations, not this.

We step through the front doors into the masquerade ball of my villainous fairytales. Dark, intricate wallpaper, parquet floors, and touches of gold pop everywhere. A grand black staircase wraps both sides of the foyer. The far doorway opens onto a room on either side and a hallway beyond, all of which are crowded with guests wearing exquisite rococo-style gowns and elaborate waistcoats and breeches, in blacks and reds and amethysts. Chandeliers and candelabras saturate the rooms with low golden light, so dark the corners cling to their secrets.

I've entered a vampire's lair. A cult's sanctuary. A haunted mansion.

And as I step inside, the thunder finally tolls a death knell in the sky and the lights flicker brighter and darker for a moment, revealing terrifying portraits and coats of armor adorned with heavy spiderwebs.

It's glorious.

The fact that my fee covered all of this?

The *ping-ping-ping* of metal against glass draws my attention to a masked woman wearing a deep violet gown on the second-floor landing above. Despite the rapid movement of her hands, I catch sight of a chain-link bracelet on her wrist. Others turn at the sound and applause breaks out, growing in a wave until every person within eyesight is looking our way and cheering.

Even if the thunder struck again, I wouldn't be able to hear it.

I glance behind me just in case someone has arrived, but Crimson and Shadow hold fast.

"This is for you, little witch," Crimson says again. "This is all for you."

That becomes crystal clear when they guide me deeper inside and every guest turns to watch us pass, crooning, "Welcome…Welcome, darling!…Welcome."

I can't believe they found so many people willing to take part in my evening, until I realize who they must be—other clients for The Company. Staff, too, probably. When I signed the contract with them, The Company specifically requested that I be willing to pay it forward in the future. I thought they meant they wanted me to recruit more members, but this is actually bigger than that.

This is orchestrated trauma. I am going to traumatize someone tonight. On purpose. And everyone here is going to help me do it. They've signed up to be accomplices.

A lick of fear races up my neck when I realize I'll be asked to do the same for some of them.

Maybe this *is* a cult and I just didn't realize when I signed up.

I mean, duh. The Company is basically a secret society, and what's that but a secular cult?

I can't regret my choice to join, though. Not when the main ballroom looks like *this*. It's the most beautiful room I've ever seen. Two walls are entirely window, the other two are covered in mirrors, and the whole space is illuminated only by dimmed wall sconces and the lightning. Silver rain cascades down the glass overhead and reflects in the mirrors so that it feels like I'm in a tent made of rain, like they've woven the storm into gossamer drapery, beaded in some places, sheer in others. A live band stands on a far stage playing one of my favorite songs, and the squeal of the electric guitar caresses my spine like soft fingernails.

It's me. This place is me.

I feel instantly at ease in a way I've never known. My dark escorts feel that shift too.

"I think she approves, Shadow," Crimson says.

Shadow runs his nose over my cheek before placing a soft kiss on my forehead and Crimson kisses my hand...

And I surrender to this. This—they—may only be mine tonight, but the night is mine too.

"Dance with me?" I ask them.

Crimson smirks and together they lead me to the center of the room where others are dancing. The others make room for us and my men sandwich me between them, pressed so tightly I can't help but giggle in apprehension. I have no idea how this is going to work.

"Follow our lead," is all Crimson says.

Then we're moving. It's like a waltz, a three-person waltz where they volley and twirl me between them in a tight circle, until the song peaks and they surround me again. We spin until we're all grinning like little kids.

It only takes three minutes to convince me it's as easy to dance with three as it is with two. I thought that might be the case all those years ago, but the night was ruined before I could find out. Which means this is another lost moment from that night years ago that The Company has set right.

When the song ends, my men take turns pulling me into their warm chests and kissing the crown of my head, whispering affections to me and each other like, "Our girl gets all the attention she wants," and, "You move so well for us."

Turns out getting everything you ever wanted is as incredible as it sounds.

And I don't think I'll ever be the same.

I can't be.

CHAPTER 8

TEN YEARS EARLIER

"She obviously lied about playing before to get you to help her."

"It's fine, babe. Don't worry about it."

"She was trying to flirt with you, Blake. Do something about it."

Emily, Blake, and Mike are losing and have been for a while. I don't know why she's acting like I'm the only one winning against them when Red-Eyes and Black-Eyes have both scored, but she is. I mean yes, once I understood the rules of beer pong, I did hit three in a row, but it's obviously beginner's luck.

Hearing Emily's loud attempt to paint me as a bad guy hurts more than I care to admit. It feels like a wire is zapping right beneath my skin. I thought she'd be impressed, maybe. I thought she'd realize I'm not the loser they always accuse me of being.

Now I'm wondering if I should miss the last shot. Or maybe I can let the guys on my team win for us so it'll take some of the heat off me.

When Red-Eyes holds up the ball, I beg, "Could you take the last shot? Please?"

He only shakes his head. "The honor is yours, little witch." Then he leans into me, lips to my ear, and says, "We destroy enemies, we don't coddle them."

His touch feels like a kiss and a promise...an offer. One

he doubles down on by staying close and placing a hand on the small of my back. He rubs a tiny circle there, confusing me more.

There's only one solo cup left, it's my turn, and I'm buzzing with excitement. I never win games. I never get to play games, but that's beside the point. It's friendly. It's fun. It's the first time in a long time I haven't tried to speed up time hoping I'd wake up in the future in a less shitty version of my life.

I don't want that to end. But I don't want to be punished for it either.

What's the right choice here? Is there one?

"Take the shot, little witch, so we can celebrate your victory," Red-Eyes says right into my ear. His warm breath scatters goosebumps across my neck. I glance at his masked face, studying his eyes. The genuine encouragement in them levels me; he actually wants me to win.

I don't even care about the game anymore; but I definitely want to celebrate with him.

Especially when Black-Eyes slides his hand into mine on the other side and nods his promise that the reward will also include him.

I put more thought into this shot than I have into my finals at school, but I have a good feeling about it as I release the ball. It hits the far edge of the solo cup and spins, rolling an inch along the very rim before it goes in.

Emily slams her hand into the side of the cup, sending it flying into the back of a girl's head a few feet away, but I'm too busy to care. Black-Eyes slides his hands across my middle, then wraps his arms around me. He lifts me off the ground and tosses me up on his broad shoulder.

My squeal is drowned out by cheers from Red-Eyes, and the graze of fingers along the back of my thighs. The touch startles me. I crane my neck to see what's happening and my heart jackhammers as I realize Red-Eyes is holding my short dress down against my legs so it doesn't ride up.

The thoughtfulness fills me with some emotion I don't know how to begin processing.

Not that I have time. Black-Eyes carries me away, and Red-Eyes follows. I catch one glimpse of Emily's seething princess brattiness—she pokes Blake in the chest—before they disappear from view.

Then we're climbing. Red-Eyes charges ahead carving a path up the dilapidated stairs through the crowd for Black-Eyes to follow. I yelp again when we reach a large hole and Black-Eyes bounds over it, holding me tightly. And I'm giggling as we reach the second floor and Red-Eyes holds open a door for us.

Black-Eyes lowers me gently, then twirls me away into Red's arms just as he shuts the door. Red dips me back while I'm still giggling and before I can say anything, his hand lifts his mask, exposing his cupid bow lips before they plow into mine.

It's a deep kiss. Slow and intense. No tongue, not even when I open my mouth in surprise. There's just a rushing scent of some sort of spiced bodywash, no doubt with a name like Hammer or Lightning or Old Cabin.

He pulls me out of the dip, still smiling.

"You were amazing down there," he says. He turns to his friend, "Tell her she was amazing."

Black-Eyes lifts the bottom of his mask, too, so his wide lips and dimpled chin are visible. His hands sweep in to cup both of my cheeks and I'm suddenly on tiptoe with a second pair of lips against mine, nibbling and teasing and tasting.

Is this real life? Maybe they dropped me through the hole in the stairs and I've already died. It'd make more sense than two guys like this *actually wanting to be here with me.*

They're not related, I don't think, but they're both tall and fit and gorgeous, at least from the neck down. Red-Eyes is slightly darker complected, a little wider but in a bodybuilder way, with beautiful hands, supple full lips, and a smile so sharp it cuts to the bone. I think he has dark hair, too, if his stubble is anything to go on. Black-Eyes is tan but lighter and wiry. His hands are larger, longer—the sort that make you feel small when he has you by the cheeks.

This whole situation is crazy. Crazy!

Verdict: I'm a bigger idiot than I originally thought.

I just let two insanely hot random strangers at a house party carry me upstairs into an empty room.

Yikes.

Yet I don't want their touch or attention to stop.

Even if it's a bad idea, which it is! Things like this don't happen to people like me. Not in my cheap, wrinkled witch costume.

Before I know it, I bounce off the wall behind me without ever becoming conscious of my retreating steps.

My nerves beat out the hungry part of me when they both step toward me. Each reaches for one of my arms. Each runs their fingers down my exposed skin, and I feel like one of those chocolate shells at a fancy restaurant that they melt by pouring molten chocolate over them to expose the dessert within. Their touch trails fire across my shell, melting my resistance until Black-Eyes slides a finger under my sleeve hem, and the shell finally gives...

Revealing a second thinner shell underneath.

"C-Can we just kiss?" I ask.

They glance at each other; the look and its meaning are a complete unknown with their masks on. But I relax a little when they both nod.

"A-And you won't tell anybody?"

Red's shoulders rise a little as he scoffs. His thumb runs across the seam of my lips. "I know you, little witch. If you want us to be your dirty little secret, that's what we'll be, but if you ask nicely, we could be so much more."

A shiver threatens to take the knees out from under me as

I study them. They must go to my school, but he doesn't sound like any of the kids I talk to sometimes. I don't recognize his voice from presentations in my classes either. It's a big school, I'm in mostly AP classes, and it'd be impossible to know for sure who they are without removing those masks, but...I don't want them to come off. I don't want to break the moment.

"What could you be?" I ask.

"Your reckoning," he says without an ounce of arrogance. In fact, he sounds like he genuinely means it. He gestures to Black-Eyes. "He saw you first in Mr. Lawson's class, but I see you clearest. We've been watching you for a very long time, waiting for a chance like this to get to know you."

I can't help but laugh a little. Mr. Lawson's class has fifty kids in it and I sit in the front row, near the door so I can leave right when the bell rings. "Watching me" is literally unavoidable in that room.

"Why haven't you talked to me at school, then?" I counter.

"You hate school," he says.

"Wrong," I say. "I'm crushing it."

I hear the smirk in his voice. "Only academically. Sometimes the things we're best at are also the things that break us. Especially when you can't escape. I won't have you associate us with that prison."

I open my mouth to call shenanigans, to tell them I'd rather have friends in prison than walk its halls alone, but he adds, "We've gone to ten shitty parties this year hoping you'd show up, but I had a good feeling about this one."

"Why?"

"You thrive in darkness, little witch. When I saw you walk through that door, all I wanted to do was talk to you, touch you, taste you."

I gulp. "And n-now that you've done that?"

He tucks a piece of my hair behind my ear, skimming his touch along my neck and under my chin, lifting it toward him.

"We want to do it again," he says, leaning in. "And then, we want to take you out for waffles. Is that all right with you?"

Joy burbles up inside of me until it reaches my lips; they curl upward at the edges before I can stop them. That sounds nice. Lovely, even.

I reach for the lowest edge of his mask and raise it just enough so his lips are visible. The ghost of a grin greets me, but I leave it for the moment to raise the mask on Black-Eyes' face too. He's panting; I can see his raging heartbeat in the vein in his neck, and his desire in the tip of his tongue as it darts out of his mouth to lick his bottom lip.

I want to tug it into my mouth, but I hesitate. Who do I kiss first?

The thought flies out of my head a second later when Red chooses for me. His fingers tug my chin back toward him and his lips crash against mine, driving me into the wall. This time, his tongue invades my mouth with a need I can feel between my legs...and in my soul.

I wish my soul would stay out of it. I don't need her getting involved. This is just a bit of fun, even if Red-Eyes kisses me like I'm the air he needs to breathe.

He breaks the connection and there's no gap at all before Black-Eyes replaces him, plunging his soft slick tongue down my throat and drawing it back slowly across mine. Crazy as it sounds, it feels like it belongs there. I miss it when it withdraws into his mouth, so I chase it with my own.

But Red-Eyes is there lifting me a second later, wrapping my legs around him, pressing me to the wall. He kisses the side of my neck while Black-Eyes plunders my mouth. It's an invasion of my senses. The plaster crumbles against my back. I can feel the cool damp of the storm seeping through the wall, but I don't care. The chill only intensifies their heat; I'm pretty sure they could keep me warm in a snowstorm. Each of them picks a side of me and their lips roam freely across my face-neck-chest while their hands wander lower to my breasts and my ass. Red moans when he grips the thickness of my thighs.

It's one of the parts of myself I've always felt a little ashamed of; I'll never have one of those little gaps between my legs that everyone seems obsessed with. I never really worried about it either, until now. Crippling uncertainty nips at me, trailing away from where he's touching me until I feel...him...harden between us so fast it drives the insecurities out of my body.

He ravages my mouth again, and when he comes up for air he growls, "God, I cannot wait for you to suffocate me with those thighs someday."

My core clenches at the promise. Maybe someday could be today.

Like it's already ingrained in me, I glance at Black-Eyes to see how he feels about that, like I need him to claim a piece of me too.

But he doesn't speak. Instead, he reaches for the top of my black dress and tugs it down until my bra's visible, and I thank whichever god monitors these sorts of things for letting me randomly pick out a nice one earlier.

Black-Eyes doesn't care about the bra. He rips down the lacy cup in half a second and sucks my nipple into his mouth. Red-Eyes does the same on the other side. Their teeth graze both sensitive peaks simultaneously and I squeeze Red so hard it's like my thighs want to cut him in half. The sight of them both there, suckling and moaning, sends me spinning.

They're not even inside me and I could go right here and—

"What's this?"

Red-Eyes' low, delighted purr pulls my attention. He's

found the tiny rose tattoo near my left shoulder, barely bigger than a dime. I had a friend do it for me last year when I thought life couldn't get any worse. It's a reminder of how hard I defended my life from the horrible invasive thoughts that threatened to take it from me.

"Is it unfinished?" he asks as Black-Eyes runs his thumb over it.

The rose is "just" a delicate black outline, but it's secretly the coolest tattoo on the planet.

"No, it's a black light tattoo," I say with a smile. "Under a black light, it glows neon pink."

Suddenly, it's like I don't even have nipples anymore. They're moist and peaked and still exposed, but the guys have forgotten them in favor of grinning at each other. I can't blame them, though; like I said, it's the coolest tattoo in the world. And it's sort of sweet that they care more about that than they do about the boobs inches from their faces.

Then they remember what they were doing. Red dips slowly, his eyes pinned to mine. His long tongue slithers out of his mouth to lick my nipple.

"You're just full of surprises," he croons.

"Yeah?"

Black-Eyes nods slowly.

My panties soak through faster than the walls of the house. That's exactly *the type of person I want to be; mysterious and capable and larger than life, not stuck in a doom spiral going nowhere fast.*

They both dart for my neck, and teeth nip my skin on both sides. I whimper knowing I'll have to wear concealer tomorrow.

"Aren't you going to ask if we're full of surprises too?" Red-Eyes teases. Even with the mask, I just know his eyebrow is arched. "If this is going to work, you really should take an interest in us. Ask us questions. Beg us to unmask ourselves."

"Yeah sure." I laugh, shoving the mask back down over his mouth. "Like this is anything other than one crazy night for any of us."

But a frown frames Black-Eyes mouth suddenly. I realize I've said something wrong when Red-Eyes sets me back down and gently tugs at my bra and dress until I'm covered again.

"Is that what you think?" He sounds hurt.

"Well, yeah. You'd never actually talk to me at school, so—"

Red-Eyes crowds me suddenly, looming. With the fake contacts and the tension I can see in his hands, he's kind of terrifying. Especially when Black-Eyes slams his hand into Red's chest to get him to take a step back.

Just like that, reality crashes back down around me. This is insanity. I shouldn't be here. I don't know these people.

Fuck, I'm stupid. Maybe I am *the piece of shit my mom thinks I am—*

I flinch at the thought, exchanging it for a healthy dose of fear and self-preservation instead.

"I'm gonna go," I say before I can chicken out.

"Wait, Ava."

Ava.

The sound of my own name out of Red's mouth is ice water through my veins. He really does *know who I am. The mortification is difficult to describe, but it's immense. Crushing.*

I dodge around him with my lips pressed together to keep the scream rushing up my throat contained. But Red-Eyes shadows me as I walk toward the door.

"There's a reason we don't talk to you. A real reason, I swear. Just hear me out—"

My mouth fills with a variety of things I want to say to him in that moment.

—I don't want to.—

—Why couldn't you just let this be what it is? Just a bit of fun.—

—I'm not sleeping with you either way, so don't bother.—

—Then you can tell me Monday. At school.—

But I don't get the chance to say any of those things. Not before the door suddenly opens and a guy wearing the same fucking unoriginal horror mask spots us. He darts inside like he's found his private party and shuts the door behind him, shooting a warm burst of air our direction, along with the distinctive scent of sage and lemon and orange.

"This is what I like to see, a real party," he sings. "I hope you saved some for me."

He steps closer in the dark room and my stomach drops as I mark the blue paint, the star on one cheek, the number 74 on the other.

Blake has found us.

CHAPTER 9

As hard as it is to believe, I hadn't thought about Emily Deutch in years before finding out about The Company. Not her specifically, anyway. She became amorphous in my mind. An inhuman monster. A boogeyman with a face that warped more and more with age into something unrecognizable.

Part of that, I know, is because I can't punish Blake for what he did to me. The possibility of justice—true lawful good justice—ended that night ten years ago.

So Emily took the brunt of that unsatisfied craving for retribution. It's not fair to her that I poured all my negative emotions into hurting her, but fuck her, it's not fair what she did to me either. And I've spent years suffering for it while she didn't suffer at all.

I learned too young that the scales don't naturally balance themselves when something horrendous happens. And that's coming from an *attorney*. Eventually, I made peace with the unfair ways of the world and learned how to live with the hypocrisy of representing white-collar criminals while hating violent criminals with a passion. There are too many assholes...just...living their lives like they haven't ruined the lives of others for any real balance to exist. And the thought of post-death hellish justice or punishment through reincarnation just doesn't make sense to me either. I don't need them punished *then* when it doesn't matter anymore;

life lessons have statutes of limitations.

Now that so much time has passed, there's only one way for Emily to truly understand how badly she hurt me.

So, a couple hours of dancing and drinking into the night when Shadow's raspy, modulated voice whispers, "She's here," in my ear, relief floods my system. It feels like I've been trapped in an elevator full of burning hot coals for years and two dashing firefighters are finally prying the door open to free me.

Crimson's hand goes to the small of my back, Shadow's to the nape of my neck, and it's more reassuring than a cozy blanket. I feel surrounded. Protected. This night won't end like the last one.

Crimson and Shadow are who Red-Eyes and Black-Eyes should have been. Everything they weren't. Everything I needed then, and now.

Their hands slide into mine and hold tightly. Crimson leads us through the mulling crowd toward the foyer.

I can tell that the vibe has shifted around us. Guests are whispering. Preparing. Their eyes dance across the three of us with encouragement. They're watching me step into position like they're living vicariously through me. They want this for me too. It fans the flame of my excitement.

But I'm still not quite prepared for the sight that greets me once we reach the hallway.

I forgot.

In the wake of Crimson and Shadow's intensity, I forgot about Sky. My third for tonight.

He steps through the front door like an anomaly, so tall it looks wrong at first glance but suits his fake name to a tee. So, too, does his mask. I had expected him to be wearing a mask as bright as a clear sunny day, but it's not. It's midnight blue and freckled with stars. Just like Crimson and Shadow, it's only a half mask and what I can see of him is gorgeous, with close-cropped curly black hair, light brown skin, a wide, distinct nose, and eyes so blue they look like gems.

"Ready?" Crimson asks.

Their presence and touch give me courage. So does the look on Sky's face when he spots us in the crowd and nods subtly. They all know their parts to play in this, and so do I.

"I'm ready."

Crimson and Shadow nod to Sky and it's like someone hit the big red detonation button. Sky's face splits into a beautiful smile that erases the darkness of a moment before. He's a great actor, whoever he is.

His head turns, he speaks to someone, and then he's moving toward us.

The crowd parts and I get my first glimpse of who he's talking to.

Her.

Princess Brat.

The Queen of Cuntiness.

The girl who ruined entire years of my life. Who made it impossible for me to know peace or trust or sexual satisfaction, like I've had her spiked collar around my neck all these years, tugging-tugging me back to that horrific night.

Emily Deutch.

She's not a girl anymore, yet she's opted for a princess gown similar to the one from back then, only even more girlish, like she can't let the past go either. There's even a tiara on her head. It takes all of half a second for me to see she's still that arrogant brat from a decade ago. Her smile is fake. Her chin is high as she glares at every other guest like she expects them to bow to her by the end of the evening.

Some do. Some play to it, and they let her catch them gawking. They're like fluffers, lifting her higher so she falls harder. I know it's terrible, but I sort of love it.

"Ooh, fabulous dress, girl!" one man croons.

She doesn't even thank him; she expects that sort of

treatment. No doubt it's been a decade more of it. I can't deny that she's just as beautiful as she was when she was in high school, and by the makeup on her face and the quality of her dress and everything, really, I can tell she's done well for herself. Probably at the expense of others.

Her bubble has never burst. Reality has never touched her.

Until now.

Sky tugs her toward us.

"Bro!" Sky says, releasing her to toss his arms around Crimson, in that handshake-hug guys like to do. Then he does the same to Shadow. "Dude, it's been too long."

"No kidding," Crimson replies. "We've missed you at poker night."

I startle. The modulation on his voice is gone; his natural timbre—like a deep cello—tickles my ears and the back of my mind...as well as other suddenly wet places.

"You can thank my queen," Sky says, tossing jazz hands at Emily like he worships the ground she walks on. "C, this is Emily. Emily, this is Crimson and Shadow. This is Crimson's house."

One of her painted eyebrows rises above the cream-colored mask that matches her dress. I raise one of my eyebrows too—is this really his home?

With a judgmental snip, Emily asks, "Crimson and Shadow? What's with the weird names?"

Crimson isn't fazed at all. "Our parents ran in the same circles as Sky's."

She does a double take at Sky. "What does that mean?"

Sky grins playfully. "Well, you know. Once you hit a certain tax bracket, if you *don't* give your kid a weird name, there's something wrong with you."

Emily doesn't seem to understand, so I offer, "Like Gwyneth Paltrow's kid—Apple, right?"

"Exactly. I know six girls named Lyre." Sky does a soft

double-take and turns toward me as if he's finally noticed me. "And who are you?"

Like sunlight breaking through the clouds, Crimson's smile breaks the intensity of his face.

"*This,*" he says, wrapping a proud arm around my shoulder and tugging me into his side, "is our girl."

Beaming with pride and warmth, Crimson presses a chaste kiss to my lips that totally surprises me in the midst of this stage play. I know he's a good actor, but I can feel his heart thrumming enthusiastically through our touch, almost like he means it—like I *am* their girl.

Shadow's there a second later, turning my chin. He kisses me, too, just as sweetly. But it's the lingering look he gives me—the gentle look in his eyes as he pulls away—that rushes blush into my cheeks. I can't help it; I press my head to the crook of his arm bashfully. Even if it's fake and even if I'm starting to crave it, his stare is too much.

So is his hand as it lands on the back of my head tenderly, and his lips as he kisses my temple.

"Aw, I knew you two were big softies," Sky says.

"You're with *both* of them?" Emily asks.

Well, she doesn't really ask it. She barks it, in disbelief, and maybe a little disgust.

No, not disgust.

When I glance her way, her sneer is one of pure jealousy.

It's an expression I've seen before—one that's haunted me. How anyone could look at her and see anything but cruelty, I've never understood; she's never tried to hide it. And I thought I was prepared to see it again, but my stomach caterwauls toward a precipice I didn't even know was inside me.

My dark protectors feel the shift. Their grips tighten around me, pulling me from the edge.

In his natural smokey coal voice, Shadow tells her, "She's our missing piece."

"Perfection," Crimson adds. "We never thought we'd get this lucky."

For a second it looks like Emily's going to say something nasty, but her expression shifts. She suddenly looks devious. I've seen that look, too, and it reminds me that they're goading her, playing their parts so well I almost believed the nice things they were saying about me.

We need her jealousy. We need her to choose to be the terrible person she was all those years ago so we can punish her for it.

In that spirit, Sky hasn't stopped staring at me since Crimson "claimed" me. And Emily's eyes narrow on him when she realizes.

"Babe, I'm thirsty," she says.

"Of course, I'll see you guys later?" Sky says to us. To me.

"We'll be around," says Crimson.

But Sky hesitates one more second, blue eyes taking me in like Emily isn't even there.

"I'm glad they finally found you," Sky says, loud enough that she can hear. "Only a special lady could handle their kind of devotion."

Then his hand slips into Emily's and they disappear into the crowd.

I take my first breath since they stepped through the door and release my tight hold on Crimson and Shadow, knowing it's crushing. If they pulled up their suits, no doubt there'd be fingermarks on their skin.

Without them to use as anchors, though, my hands tremble violently.

I don't know why their touch hid my body's reaction from me. Could they feel my body shaking the entire time? Was I as easy to read as a neon bar sign? How am I going to go through with the rest of tonight if *talking* to her is too much?

But the second we break contact, they're both in front of

me, looming over me, blocking the entire party from view. They pull me in, pressing my head to the place where their arms touch. We're like a little private archipelago in the chaos.

"Just breathe," Crimson coaches, running his warm hand down my spine over and over.

"You did so well," Shadow says, his hand cupping the nape of my neck lovingly.

This is a play. *A play*, I remind myself as I pull back to look them in the eye. They're just good guys helping me.

"I'm sorry for breaking character," I whisper.

"Hey," Crimson whispers back. "You're allowed to feel anything you're feeling. We *want* you to feel everything. We're here to care for you."

I laugh internally at that. Apparently, they gave me therapy escorts…although I guess all sex workers are therapists in their own way.

"You've already done so much," I squeak. "I know I'm a lot. I don't want to burden you."

"You have *never* been a burden," Crimson says through gritted teeth, and I almost believe him. "There's nothing we wouldn't do for you."

In echo, Shadow cups my cheeks and kisses me softly again, eyes imploring. I love the intensity in them.

"We're yours," Shadow whispers against my lips.

"Your darkest wish is our command," Crimson adds.

"I think I need a drink," I admit.

Shadow nods, planting one more kiss on me before he's gone.

Then, it's just Crimson and me. There's no awkwardness at all, only his dark half-grin as he studies my face. It disappears quickly though, replaced by something that looks like pain as he runs his thumb across the back of my hand.

"Don't get comfortable with me, little witch," he warns suddenly. "I don't deserve your trust yet, remember. Wait until I do things right this time."

I fight the smile that threatens to surface. He's right. I'm jumping the gun. I'm fast forwarding through my own fantasy. At this point ten years ago, I was on edge around Red-Eyes… and he hadn't even hurt me yet.

So why, then, do I feel like I can trust Crimson *beyond* the part he's playing? Maybe because it doesn't feel like a part. Not exactly. There are little reminders that he's been hired for this, but there have been just as many to suggest he did his own research. He went above and beyond to prepare—the words he shouldn't know, the sincerity of his heartbeat.

I know I can't read anything into it, though. I only get him for one night.

He seems determined to remind me that this is fiction a second later when he asks, "Ready for the next stage?"

Oh am I. I've been preparing for this.

"The question, Crimson, is whether *you* are."

Like some sort of dark creature, he bares his teeth in a dazzling smile that has my abdomen clenching on itself. Our time in the car wasn't enough. I need more of him so badly. More of them both.

Maybe he can sense it because he suddenly says, "We need a bathroom."

His warm, calloused hand slides into mine and he tugs me deeper into the house. He removes a red rope barring a second, tucked away staircase and leads me up to a deserted section of the second floor. It's just as beautiful as it is downstairs, with the addition of more comfort. Like this is where people *actually* live.

"Are we allowed up here?"

His lips quirk. "Of course. This is my house."

"Really? I thought you were just saying that."

A flood of questions races for my mouth. Questions about The Company, his background outside of this charade tonight. Does he know the Shadow actor outside of this? Does The Company use them as a pair often for women's fantasies? I don't know if I'm allowed to know any of that, but I'm dying to ask. If this house—this *palatial mansion*—isn't a rental, then Crimson is filthy rich. Why would he need to act as an escort at all? Or is he so good at pleasuring people that he makes this kind of money?

Mmm. I hope so.

And what if he *isn't* an escort at all? Is he just…a guy willing to go along with this because The Company asked him to? If everyone here tonight is a former client of The Company what kind of fantasy would someone with Crimson's money need them to make happen that he couldn't make happen for himself? Maybe he's a famous actor. Maybe this is an acting exercise for him? Or maybe men really *are* just cool with being paired off together to fuck a stranger.

I don't get the chance to ask any of those questions, though, as he opens the door ahead of me and ferries me into a stunning bedroom. It's enormous and grandiose with a four-poster canopy bed to match and a giant armoire so large I think several people could hide in it. There are also two enormous mullioned windows overlooking the rose garden, which still glows neon in the darkness. In the time I've been here, the storm has only worsened, so the outside world through the window looks like an abstract watercolor.

But I get distracted by a tiny detail I wasn't expecting. The walls wear a dark charcoal embossed wallpaper with a repeating motif of roses and masks. I can't help but run my fingers across the textured surface. The chances that this pattern is a coincidence is slim to none—they really *did* go all out for this.

"Do you like it?" Crimson asks.

I glance back to find him practically pressed against me, breathing down my neck. God, I love when he's this close.

The temptation to touch him is so strong I feel like my soul is being tested somehow.

"Are you kidding? It's like someone walked into my head and brought my dreams to life."

"Good, it took me weeks to get it ready for you."

It's statements like that that are fucking with my head. It's not a necessary thing to say; it's not a scripted line integral to the plot of this fantasy. And it's so easy to misinterpret. I know he's just saying my fantasy was so specific it took him a while to get the details right, not that he did this *for me* personally...

But he seems to want to keep me on the edge of wondering.

Crimson suddenly grabs my hand and pulls me into the adjoining bathroom, which is larger than the first studio apartment I ever rented. Then he grabs my hips and slides me up onto the dark marble counter beside the double sinks. A giggle of nerves erupts out of me...right before his hands slide into place around my neck and his mouth claims mine. Tongues tangle. Lips part in heated, needy gasps. Crimson groans and it sounds like a roar so close to my ear—one that summons a wave of hot wetness between my legs. His grip on my throat tightens and he pulls me toward him, his hard body, demanding that I wrap myself around him, cling to him, so I do.

I want close.

No, fuck close.

I want inseparable.

I remind myself that I *must* submit to this. I must stop questioning, stop taking myself out of the moment. Tonight, I need the real world to fade away. I need reality to end at the door. So I refuse to question why he's brought me up here. Or why he seems so genuinely hungry for me. Desperate for my touch. His eyes search my face like it holds the answer to an unspoken question. Like he'll brand my face with the answer he wants if he doesn't find it there already.

But he's holding back. He wants me so badly. Every inch of his body language tells me he does. From the hands he keeps wrapped around my throat, pushing me away a little even while his hips press deeper against my center. To the cock he rubs against my wet pussy, how it jerks a little with each pass, up and down. He's denying me while refusing to let me go. And I'm the same, caught in a moment where I might claw to keep him close or claw to keep him away. It's a tug of war between us that neither of us wants to win.

"We have to stop before I make you mine right here right now," he growls, teasing my bottom lip between his teeth.

It's only when he pulls away that I realize how entangled I was with him. I literally have to pry my own hands apart so he can take a step back. Embarrassment streaks through me like an icy comet momentarily, until I see the panting elation on his face. Until he kisses me again, humming with delicious anticipation.

"God, I've missed you, my little witch."

It's theater. It's fantasy. It's fiction.

"I missed you, too, Red-Eyes," I admit, sliding my hand into his dark hair, teasing it between my fingers, punctuating my words with little kisses across his lips. "I haven't been able to stop thinking about you since that night. Every time I was with someone else, I imagined they were you. Every time I touched myself, I thought of your hand there."

His grip tightens on my throat. "Fuck, you have no idea how long I've waited to hear you say that."

I expect another kiss, hard and brutal and needy, but it doesn't come. Instead, I realize Crimson's eyes are squeezed shut just as his grip on my throat loosens and he steps back, catching his breath. The chill of his distance settles across my heated skin like frost—I hate it.

"I have to make you ready for the both of us."

"Oh, I'm ready," I assure him.

He smirks and grips my hips again, pulling me off the sink onto my feet, flat against his broad chest, trapping me against the counter. There's no air to breathe except his air, no space to move except closer to him. When he tugs my chin higher to look him in the eye, the darkness I find there envelops me.

"Have you been with multiple men at the same time before?" He says it as a question, but with a tone that suggests he already knows the answer. "Have you ever been filled completely?"

"N-No," I admit. "But I've done all the moves individually."

"Even though you needed more than one man to satisfy you?"

"I…" I decide to tell him the truth. "I wanted to wait for you."

My statement seems to hit him hard. I can almost feel his blood begin to race through our touch, and some mad expression—of ecstasy, of excitement—streaks across his face.

Then suddenly, I'm turning. My reflection in the mirror greets me for a split second before his hand splays wide on my back and pushes my chest into the counter. I'm suddenly an inch from the marble that's still warm from where my ass was sitting on it.

His hands lower to the hem of my dress.

They tease the fabric higher until the chill of the bathroom caresses my nearly bare ass.

"Fuck," he murmurs, gripping both of my cheeks with his hands. "Fucking beautiful. Your phat ass is so juicy, baby."

Baby? I guess he didn't get the same rules and warnings I did.

I think he should have because my heart, my stomach, my cunt all tighten at the dark, molasses-y quality of the soft word spoken by his voice. Fuck, it's been so long since I had anyone to call me baby, I forgot how good it sounded to be wanted.

"Hold your dress up," he whispers breathlessly. "Stay just like that."

I turn my head a little at the sound of a drawer opening, but I can't see what he's doing. I hear a quick *click* and suddenly a warm liquid drizzles down the valley below my tailbone.

It surprises me, I jerk with surprise. "Crimson?"

"Relax. You need this," is all he says before his finger slides to my back entrance and barges right in.

"Whoa!" I can't help it. My natural instinct is to squirm, even though his intrusion feels good—great—especially when paired with his breathless aching groan and the way his other hand squeezes my ass like he's so excited he can barely hold himself back.

He presses his hand firmly down onto my lower back, holding me in place as he slips a second lubricated finger in. "Let me take care of you. I'll go slow for you now…Later, well…"

Later. Right, this is only the beginning. This is probably nothing compared to what's to come.

Slowly, he massages, slipping his fingers deeper, then pulling back, then deeper again. After a moment, his other hand leaves my cheek and more lube drizzles down onto the hole.

He takes his time worshipping my ass. And I do mean worship. His breathless gasps have become groans have become murmured exclamations. "So beautiful. So fucking sexy."

My eye catches his in the mirror's reflection and I realize, while his fingers are slowly invading my body, his eyes are darting between that part of me…and me. He's watching me, watching my mouth as I tuck my lips between my teeth.

And when he realizes I'm watching him?

"You'll look so beautiful sandwiched between us, baby. Especially after we catch you."

My stomach tightens dangerously at the thought…and he feels it through our touch. A smile erupts onto his face sharp enough to cut. His hand snakes around my throat from behind and he pulls me up slightly away from the counter before taking my mouth with his.

And holy fuck.

There's something about the feel of his tongue and his fingers…

Plunging in and out in tandem…

His desperate whispered growl against my bruised, hungry mouth…

It sends a quake through my core strong enough to level a building. Shaking. I'm shaking, clinging to his arm, wondering what life could possibly look like after this. How will *anyone* measure up to this intensity? Who cares if he's an actor—give him the damned Oscar.

"That's perfect, little witch. Just like that." His voice laps at the edges of my sanity; he sounds just as sated as I am, but I haven't even touched him yet—

The thought of reaching for him is violently ejected from my mind the second I feel his fingers pull out of my ass and something smooth and soft and coated with lube replaces them.

He doesn't hesitate.

He doesn't give a warning.

His hand leaves my throat to hold me down again as a thick…thing…nudges through the entrance his fingers just relaxed and slips inside with a fullness I can feel in my throat.

"What the fuck, Crimson!"

"I told you, you'll need this," he says with a chuckle. Then he slaps my butt playfully as something plastic-y nudges into alignment with the crack of my ass. "Stand up."

I...

I slowly raise my torso, feeling my way through the strange intrusion. It's not uncomfortable; it's more the thought of it that makes me pause. Like feeling something between your toes you know isn't supposed to be there. Except it's not my toes, it's my asshole stretched wide by a...

"I bought this specially for you," Crimson says, turning me so that I can glance over my shoulder at the butt plug now lodged inside me. A purple T-shaped handle is tucked between my cheeks with a little rhinestone rose right at the center. It's actually sort of pretty.

"You could have told me."

"And ruin the look on your face?" He chuckles. "Never."

Pfft. "Oh please, I imagine you're going to see me plenty surprised tonight."

"Baby, you have no idea," he purrs, pulling me in for another slow, teasing kiss...one that makes me aware of how often suddenly full parts of my body clench every time he touches me. "This is only a starter size, so you're still in for a big surprise later when we take turns filling you."

It shouldn't sound sweet—he's talking about ravaging me and probably ruining all sexual encounters for me in the future. And yet, his darkened eyes almost glow with warmth.

I don't want to break the mood, but I'm just so relieved how utterly perfect he's been so far.

"Thank you for thinking of this," I say. "It's really...considerate."

"I'm going to enjoy watching you walk around in it," he teases.

The look in his eyes, the feel of this new tension in my body, this promise of fullness—it's a perfect moment. One that has me almost forgetting what's to come...

Until he says something that leaves me utterly confused.

"Just remember, we never wanted to hurt you," he says, his lips tipping down into a soft frown. "Not back then, not tonight, and not tomor…"

His voice cuts out a second before I swear he's going to say *tomorrow*, but there *is* no tomorrow.

I open my mouth to ask but he beats me to it.

"You ready for the next stage?"

"Of course. This is the easy part," I reply, because it's true. The next phase of this fantasy is pure self-indulgence. It's my chance to right an entire childhood of wrongs—of bullying, of mockery, of self esteem eroded by circumstance and people like Emily Deutch.

Crimson guides me back downstairs, indulging my very slow walk as I adjust to the secret passenger inside me. My waddle seems to amuse him.

Shadow finds us as soon as we enter the ballroom.

"Everything okay?" he asks.

"Just peachy," Crimson says with a smirk…and I don't know if it's an inside joke between them or what but Shadow literally blushes. He hands me the drink he fetched me, then steps behind me as we walk; I can almost feel his heated gaze on my ass, like he suddenly can't tear his eyes away from it. Then his hand is there, massaging one of my cheeks. When I glance back at him, the look on his face is so beautiful I can barely stand it. The shadowy hunger. The impatient petulance, like he's playfully upset he missed what Crimson did to me.

Crimson seems to sense it, "Don't sulk. *You* get to take it out."

Shadow looses a growl I feel in my diaphragm right before he dives for my neck and suckles, humming.

"Is that what you want, sweetheart?"

Sweetheart?

"Yes please."

I feel Shadow's teeth graze my skin once more before he

pulls away. "God, I'm going to make you feel so good tonight."

"First things first," Crimson says, pulling our attention back to the room and the rest of my fantasy.

The ballroom is so crowded now, there's almost no space to dance at all…not that I could with this thing inside me. Crimson's hand goes to my other cheek almost possessively as they guide me to a slightly elevated area near the room's massive fireplace. From here, anyone who enters will see the band first, me second.

As I hit my mark, with my men to either side of me, the crowd slightly parts, revealing Sky and Emily dancing on the dance floor. They're having a grand ole time…letting Emily show off. Despite the heavy crowds, and the fact that everyone around them is only taking up the space they need to enjoy the night, she's purposefully taking up as much space as possible. Lashing out, almost. She's almost forcing people to back up or move off the floor so she doesn't hit them, because she's *trying* to.

It was always difficult to explain to my therapist what she was really like all those years ago, but if I could record this moment and show it to her, she might finally understand. Emily Deutch doesn't just have Main Character Syndrome, she's one of those people who tries to warp reality to fit the version of the world they prefer to live in. Suppose we all do that to a certain extent, but we usually stop when it starts to hurt other people.

Not her.

As I watch, she forces Sky to twirl her away from him. But she continues the twirl far beyond the force he put behind it…until she slams into a dancing pair nearby. One of them genuinely yelps and staggers and Emily prances back to Sky without a care in the world.

I don't know what's wrong with her, but seeing her enjoy herself at others' expenses genuinely makes my skin crawl.

Her godawful cruel smile brings the worst moment of my life racing back to the surface of my mind. I don't realize my own body language is all but projecting my inner turmoil to the room until Shadow's hand slides into my hair.

He leans in to be heard over the music, "What's wrong?"

Crimson jerks at the sound of his voice and he's suddenly there too, hands on my waist, beautiful eyes staring into my soul.

"She's a nightmare," I say, because I don't know how else to describe how it feels to watch her like this.

"She always was," Shadow says. "I can't tell you how many times I've thought of ending her life for you. If we had been able to find you before now, I would have—"

Shadow's voice dies as he glances at Crimson. I turn to look too, surprised by the dark expression on his face—guilt, anger, warning.

But this is *my* fantasy; I want to know. "What would you have done, Shadow?"

Tearing his gaze from Crimson, he tells me, "I would have given you what you needed years ago. You wouldn't have needed The Company to deliver her to you."

"Shadow!" Crimson barks.

Shadow doesn't back down. Darkened gaze upon me, he adds, "We've been looking for you since that night, and if it had been up to me, we would've spent the last ten years making our mistakes up to you."

Crimson's hand lands on Shadow's shoulder like a vice and yanks him slightly behind me. His mouth lurches toward Shadow's ear and faintly I hear, "You're ahead of schedule. Cut it out."

I open my mouth to assure Crimson, it's okay if they jumped to the wrong page in their script—Shadow's words are the exact sort of balm I need right now before everything kicks off—but I don't get the chance.

All at once, the pre-amble to tonight's main event begins.

You wouldn't notice it unless you were really paying attention, but the band's volume lowers. Lights in certain areas of the room dim, others brighten.

"Darling! There you are!"

The voice belongs to a guest with a thick black beard wearing a purple gown and eyeshadow to match. They throw their hands up and make a show of their entrance, drawing attention in their wake as they beeline straight for me.

"Hi gorgeous!" I wrap my arms around them like we've known each other for years. "Thank you so much for coming!"

"Anything for you, pet!"

As they move on, other guests filter my way, practically *lunging* for my attention while Crimson and Shadow guard me, effortlessly shifting between pure adoration toward me, and palpable threat toward everybody else.

It's a nonstop barrage of people I've never met greeting me like I'm their best friend for almost an hour. In between and around each guest, Crimson and Shadow dote on me. A quick kiss on my cheek, a whisper in my ear that makes me laugh. One pulls back only for the other to draw me in and I can't help but play into these tiny moments. I want to. I tease and kiss and whisper back whenever there's an empty second. It feels like a mini-game, and I relish the fact that I seem to be winning, outdoing my two players, surprising them as often as they surprise me.

But of course, the best part is watching Emily slowly lose her ever-loving mind across the room.

Her tells are small at first. She can't quit looking at us. She starts getting upset any time one of the people in the group she's speaking with motions that they'll be right back and then comes to say hello to me. Each time, I can almost see her teeth grinding with disbelief and frustration.

It only gets better when she tries to find a new group, only for the exact same thing to happen again. One person even pulls at Emily's arm, trying to get her to join her pilgrimage to greet me. I almost give the game away when she yanks out of the woman's grasp and I burst out laughing.

Her anger is delicious. Practically nutritious. It feeds me, nourishing the wounded kid in me who went so long uncared for.

Maybe I should feel bad on some level, but her discomfort is entirely her doing. She could simply not care and let the night go on without her, but she can't. I knew she wouldn't be able to. If she could, none of this would be necessary.

That's the beauty of tonight. Her fate is in her own hands and she doesn't even know it. If she doesn't transgress, I can't punish her.

But it's our job to push the issue.

Nothing quite grinds Emily's gears like Sky's wayward attention. He keeps peeking at me and finding reasons to look this way. For a while, I don't look at him at all. Not directly. As more and more people come to say hello, I get glimpses of him ogling me, at Emily staring at me, growing madder and madder.

Until finally, for the fun of it, I wave at him. It's a tiny gesture, simply acknowledging his existence. His lips quirk into a grin. He raises his hand to wave back and—

Emily smacks his arm so hard I actually hear it over the music. Suddenly, she's berating him. Her finger stabs right into his diaphragm to punctuate whatever she's saying.

My hand drops and guilt seeps into me like water dampening a sock.

Not for her, but for him. Obviously. I don't want him to be hurt in this, not even a little bit. I don't think that's part of this; signing up to participate in one of these doesn't mean you can be mistreated. At least, it shouldn't. Then again, if The Company pulled out the stops like this for me…

"Here we go," Crimson says, drawing my attention back to Emily and Sky. "Brace yourself."

I barely look up in time to see Emily marching toward me, glass of wine in hand.

I know this has to happen.

I know this is the moment she seals her fate. But it's her fate to seal.

So, I let my lips curve upward as she approaches and I say, "Emily, hi again—" right before she tosses her full glass of wine straight in my face.

CHAPTER 10

TEN YEARS EARLIER

Blake's presence in the room doesn't register for a long moment. I just stand there, tucked between Red-Eyes and Black-Eyes, absorbing Blake's arrival in a detached sort of way. Just like I would any kid coming in and out of a room at school. He has nothing to do with me.

But I realize I'm wrong half a second later when I step around him, headed for the exit. Blake shifts sideways like a sliding door, putting himself right in my path of escape.

"Where are you going?" His tone is laughing, but it's not a joke.

"I'm leaving."

I try stepping around him again, but he's there before I even raise my foot. "Don't run away. I just got here."

I've never been very good with social cues. I think maybe I just haven't had enough experience with them. Other people. The weird things they do.

Or maybe it's that there are just certain things I would never do to somebody else, so when they happen to me...I just...glitch. I try to misremember it.

Blake's hand rises before I even notice it. It's there, sliding over my chest, squeezing, groping in the blink of an eye. Even then, I step back, as if it was my mistake being too close.

But then he pinches my nipple almost to bruising as if to hold me in place and his other hand is on my butt squeezing.

His voice rumbles, "Hey, be nice."

And a gurgled yelp escapes me, as if at least one part of my body is offended on my behalf. As if at least one part is reminding me I should be offended.

"Don't touch me, you creep!"

Even though the words are softly said, I shove him back with a force that surprises us both. My hands shake a little in surprise too. My heart, well, it's sprinting in my chest, telling me to gtfo.

But I'm frozen as Blake steps toward me again. And in the split second between him reaching me and trying to flee, two blurs of anger barrel past me on either side. I completely forgot Red-Eyes and Black-Eyes were there in the moment, but they shove Blake into the wall so hard, it crumples like wet paper behind him.

Uncertain relief trickles through me for a moment, along with some quiet hotter emotion I've never felt before. They're...defending me.

Blake shoves himself out of the hole in the wall and rises to face them, and for a second, I think Red and Black-Eyes are on my side.

"Take another step," Red says. "Take another step, we dare you."

But...then Blake taps Red's stomach playfully, and his hand lands on Black-Eye's shoulder.

Blake's voice dances with laughter as he says, "I'm just messing with you, man. We can take turns, it's cool. You can go first."

My soul curdles with dread. I've been alone all my life, really, but this... I suddenly feel a loneliness so rotten I want to puke.

My foot catches as I take a step back and I stumble as I rush for the door.

"Ava, wait!"

I don't. Why would I? My hand lands on the doorknob

like it's the padlock on my cell in a sinking ship. If I don't get out of here I'm going to drown. Or worse.

But worse is waiting for me on the other side.

Emily—Princess Brat herself—stands a foot away in the crowded hallway with her hand raised as if she was two seconds from opening the door herself. She glares at me like I'm a bit of gunk on her shoe for a long moment, until her head tilts to look past me...and sees the three guys there.

"Blake?" The name leaves her throat in a growl of accusation. But there's no chance for him to speak. The moment I move to dart around her, her angry eyes snap to me. "You little whore."

"I didn't—"

"You fucking slut!"

Knee-jerk reaction, I blurt, "Nothing happened!"

But Blake is like a man with a mouth on autopilot. "Baby, you know she's just a worthless thot. A piece of trash. She meant nothing to me."

I hear movement in the room behind me—and it's my cue to leave.

I brush past Emily. I barely make it a foot before clawed fingers scrape my neck and yank at my hair and the fabric of my dress. A scream bursts from me unbidden and the party freezes around us. The thirty people or so on this level are suddenly our captive audience.

And I realize a moment too late that Emily might be mad, but...she loves attention more than her own anger. This shift in the house around us is like a match to kindling for her.

"Do you know who I am?" she whispers into my hair.

"Let go!"

Claws scratch my face as she scrapes my mask off, exposing me to the entire party.

"I should have known... Ava Dillard. Trailer trash loser just like your mother." She shoves me away so hard I clatter to my knees in a heap on the wet, gross floor. "Hey

everybody. The village bicycle thought she could steal my man! I'll give a backstage pass to one of my brother's concerts to anyone who brings me a piece of her clothing tonight."

CHAPTER 11

Emily's cackle echoes loudly through the ballroom as the band cuts its song short.

"You should fix your face, bitch," she says, as I stand up and try to wipe the wine out of my stinging eyes. "Your paint job's ruined."

Shadow and Crimson are there a second later with handkerchiefs, bodies tight and thrumming with anger I can feel in the heat around them both, but neither makes a move toward her—it's not time yet.

"Is there a problem?" I ask, so politely, as the last drip of wine is wiped away.

"You think I didn't see you checking out my man? What? Two isn't enough for you?"

"What man?" I tease, scanning the crowd playfully before I land on Sky. "That one?"

This time, I don't just wave at him. I twizzle my fingers a little in a *come hither* gesture that's almost royal in its unhurried elegance—

"Bitch, do you *want* to start something?" Emily's voice cuts like a straight razor. She's suddenly inches from me, so close I can feel her breath against my cheek...

And that's when I strike. My hand is in her hair, coiling the mass into a tight tangled ball in my fist, yanking her head back at a cruel angle, before she can even whimper.

"Ow!" she squeals, voice laced with genuine hurt. "What

the fuck are you doing!"

I almost laugh at her. "You asked if I wanted to start something. I'm giving you my answer."

"Let go, you psycho!"

"Psycho? Psycho!" I have fun screaming it right in her face...for the drama, you know. "Did you hear that? The guest who entered our home and threw wine in my face called me a psycho."

Shadow's voice rumbles like thunder, "I heard her loud and clear."

I glance at him. "Babe, do you think I'm a psycho?"

His eyes whip to meet mine, twinkling with some unexpected joy. A smile as dark as midnight curves his face. "Oh, I hope so."

I stammer for a moment. I knew he would play along, but that look in his eye—it seems so real!

Suddenly, there are lips against the back of my head and Crimson is there against my ear as I turn to him and Emily. "I dunno. You haven't even clawed her eyes out yet, baby. I think you're a saint."

"Is that what you want me to be?" I ask him. I'm not even sure why, but I want to know.

He doesn't hesitate. "Only when you feel like it."

"And if I want to be bad?"

"Ooh." Crimson's laugh is a low purr. "You know my favorite color's red, baby."

His words are a release. Permission he knows I don't require, but need in the moment. I don't know why but it loosens some hidden string in me that was wound too tight.

It does the opposite to Emily. I think in the few seconds I've been talking with my guys, she's realized something's wrong here. Not a single person at the party has moved since the music died. The hundreds-strong crowd is merely watching the play unfold like an audience of statues.

Emily whimpers as it hits her, how royally fucked she is.

Suddenly one of her hands rises with the wine glass as if she's about to stab it right into my eye—but Shadow's there, slamming it out of her hand a second later. And Crimson's hands twist her arms behind her back so hard she squeals again with actual pain.

"Easy, Crimson," I say, not taking my eyes off her. Her face is barely inches from mine. "Just hold her still for me."

"I'll do more than that," he growls against her ear.

"Sky, baby? Help me!"

All four of us turn to find him there, three feet or so away, watching. Stiff, hesitant discomfort practically ripples through his body. Concern has him raising his hands as if he's entered a hostage negotiation.

"Let's talk about this," Sky says.

"Get this freak off me!" Emily screeches louder.

"What would you like to talk about?" I ask Sky.

"Maybe you could let her go?" he asks, and for a second he sounds so genuinely worried, my grip loosens in her hair, wondering if he thinks I'm pushing things too far.

But then Emily ruins her own rescue, "God Sky, you're such a fucking little pussy. Push this bitch off me! Kick their asses! Do something, you spineless loser!"

"You gonna let her talk to you like that, bro?" Crimson asks.

"You could get better ass anywhere," Shadow says.

Emily stiffens. "Fuck you!"

"I would," I say. "You're gorgeous, Sky. I could please you in ways Emily could never dream of."

I say it to keep the ruse going, to keep the tension high, but I feel a flinch through Emily's body from Crimson, and Shadow suddenly scooches closer to me, almost in surprise. As if I caught them off-guard. Which is a little odd considering I'm meant to have all three of them tonight; Sky was always part of the plan, even if I sort of forgot about him while I was sandwiched between my two dark escorts.

Some strange sense of guilt curls around me and I turn quickly to Crimson, in apology.

"I meant he could join us," I assure him. "Only if you want. I know he's your friend and you trust him." I turn to Shadow and add, "Only if my guys are okay with it?"

I raise my brow at Shadow and wait...but he only nods. And when he nods, it's a tepid, begrudging gesture, like he *really* doesn't mean it.

I press my face to his suit, nuzzling, for reassurance. He wraps his arms around me in answer, but through his touch I can feel the truth of his hurt in the pounding of his heart. I...actually upset him.

That's not what I wanted to do.

Crimson pushes things along. "What do you say, Sky?" He wiggles Emily a little as he holds her wrists at her back. "You want this piece of trash or you ready to trade up for perfection?"

"You know what?" Sky says. "I am."

"Sky!" Emily barks.

"I need a woman who can treat me right, not some worthless thot who thinks she's queen of the universe."

"Can you be loyal to me?" I ask.

"If that's what you want."

"Prove it," I say.

With that, I nod to Crimson, and together we shove Emily away. She stumbles down the stairs and clatters to her knees on the marble below, just catching herself on her wrists. The closest guests recoil a little, until there's a halo of empty space around her.

"Show me how much she means to you," I say. "Show me what she's worth."

CHAPTER 12

TEN YEARS EARLIER

I'm on my knees where Emily threw me. The upstairs hallway is partially carpeted, but the carpet is old and wet and gross against my skin where I'm curled in a ball on the floor, anticipating the worst from the kids around me.

It's only a matter of time before they hurt me, I just know it. I can feel it in the air like electricity before a storm. The real storm outside cackles as if it's watching our drama too.

Emily's voice rings out, piercing and cruel. "I said this fucking hog thought she could steal my man, people! Backstage pass for a piece of clothing. It's the size of a circus tent so there's plenty to go around."

"Please, Emily, I didn't do anything!" I almost screech.

"Starting now, bitches!"

Nobody moves a muscle. I mean, I'm not looking up, but no one touches me. I-I don't know why they're not leaping to follow her command, but gratitude swells inside me.

"Hello! Did anybody hear me?!" she shouts again.

Footsteps sound to my left and I flinch closer to the floor, waiting for the worst.

Instead, a hand ducks into view, palm up, in offer.

"Here, it's okay," some guy says.

I don't...know if I can trust it...but I have to. I have to get out of here.

Shaking, my fingers land against his palm and I move to stand, mouth already forming the words "Thank you" before

I'm fully off the floor…but the words die as I look up and realize who saved me.

It's not some Good Samaritan.

It's not somebody I know well.

It's Mike. The guy Emily drove here.

His voice carries as he says, "I'll take that action," and suddenly…unceremoniously, grips the neckline of my dress with both of his hands and rips it right down the middle. He only barely misses grabbing my bra. But what does that matter?

As tears flood my eyes, other hands are there around me, touching me, grabbing me, groping me, tearing at the dress I can't keep around my body, ripping it into pieces so small I couldn't even press them against myself to cover anything.

I push. I shove. I scrape somebody.

But it's not enough.

I beg. I plead. I wail with humiliation.

They ignore me. Laughter rings out from somewhere as the dress pieces yank free of their seams and I'm left in my bra, underwear, tights, and shoes, leaving barely anything to the imagination.

And then I hear the click of someone's cell phone camera. It breaks me. It's the worst sound I've ever heard and all I can do is keep my head down, my eyes on the ground and—

"That's only one piece, idiots!" Emily sneers. "Where's the rest of it!"

My breath hitches with panic when a hand reaches right into the back of my tights without hesitation. And I do the only thing I can think to do.

I shove them so hard, I almost topple over with them. As I feel someone at my back, I spin with my hand already extended. My knuckles connect with their jaw hard enough it feels like bone on bone.

And I'm moving. Running. Dodging. Body checking. Anything to reach the stairs. Anything to reach the door.

"Stop her!"

"Grab her!"

There are too many hands. Too many arms. Too many bodies suddenly in my way.

The tights rip down the back and I'm on my knees again.

My shoes are ripped off my feet.

My socks too.

A fist twists in the elastic of my old ratty bra and tears, even as I scream, "PLEASE!"

The underwear was already on its last leg—I'd had it on my list to buy new ones next time I got a paycheck. Now I'll have to. The fabric tears from my body like tissue paper.

Laughter.

Catcalls.

Fingers.

It's a nightmare.

A nightmare!

And I don't know where to go...

Until my outstretched hand grips polished wood, and I realize it's the lip of the top stair. The stairs! I curl my other hand around it and drag my body between someone's legs.

I scramble off the second floor landing just as someone reaches for my ankle...but I overcorrect. I can't help it. I hit someone on the stairs, bounce away...and then I'm falling through the gaping hole Black-Eyes once leapt over. And a circle of faces peer down at me from above, retreating every second, as I fall into oblivion.

CHAPTER 13

"Go on, Sky," I tell him. "Show me you're done with this worthless thot."

"Babe, wait," Crimson says, and the party holds on his word. "That dumb skank thought she could come here tonight and do whatever she wanted, but this isn't her party. It's yours."

His head turns to the assembled masses and adds, "Fifty bucks to whoever brings me a piece of this crazy bitch."

Crimson's voice barely quiets before Shadow says, "Whoa, whoa!" as if he's disgusted by the idea. But he's not. Far from it. "Fifty bucks? For this piece of trash? Twenty max, bro."

A voice calls out from the crowd. "I'll do it for ten, honey!"

"*What is WRONG with you people?!*" Emily's preaching to the choir. She's barely on her feet before someone behind her yanks out an entire tendril of her hair, right out of her scalp as if they're yanking out an extension.

It…catches me off-guard, I'm not going to lie. I wasn't expecting it. I wasn't expecting pain, only humiliation.

But before I can speak, Sky's there beside Emily. "Sky, we have to get out of here. Please, get me out of here! These people are crazy."

He cups her face so gently, it's almost sweet until…

"Baby, crazy is thinking that justice won't cut a bitch."

"…Huh?"

With that, one of Sky's hands lands on the neckline of her gown and *wrenches* at the fabric, tearing a massive swatch away, exposing the see-through petticoat underneath.

"What are you doing!" Her scream could wake the dead.

But Sky turns to me. "Is this enough?"

Soaking in the moment, I shake my head slowly. Pointedly.

And all hell breaks loose. The mob descends on her like they're a pack of crazed zombies hungry for fabric rather than flesh. Emily literally disappears from view as gown confetti decorates the air.

It's the moment I've waited nearly ten years for.

It's all I've ever dreamed it would be.

It's delicious. It's just. It's a soothing hug for the soul.

I only wish I could see more of the action; there are just too many enthusiastic bodies in the way.

After a few moments, though, the crowd parts. The few people who managed to hold onto their pieces of Emily wave the petticoats and shoes and several more pieces of her hair like victory flags.

And the boogeyman who's chased me for a decade is there in a naked little ball on the floor. Crying her little wolf-in-sheep's-clothing tears. Trembling like the useless autumn leaf she is.

I wait for sympathy to come. I pause to let my mind drum up some sort of remorse.

But this is nothing. *Nothing* compared to what she did that night. What she inspired. What happened *after* I was stripped of my dignity at that party.

Then a new sound—one I've never heard before—catches my attention. A laugh leaves Shadow's mouth and it sounds how I imagine Death's laugh would, dark and low and indifferent.

It's echoed by someone else nearby. Then someone else.

Before I know it, the entire party—including Sky, including Crimson—has joined in, mocking her as they point and taunt and toss the pieces of her dress at her.

The brutal jeering cacophony at Emily's expense massages away all the knots and bruises and scars that night long ago left with me. Well, almost all of them.

I wish I could record it and fall asleep to it.

I wish I could baptize myself in it.

I wish it was enough.

CHAPTER 14

TEN YEARS EARLIER

When my back slams into the dark wooden floor beneath the stairs, it's the dampness alone that saves me from shattering. I hear the wood crack beneath me, feel it tear lightly at my skin where the boards are rough, but otherwise, it's only soreness I know I'll feel tomorrow.

A sound rouses me to my feet—the stampede of dozens of people down the staircase overhead, coming for me.

I'm in some sort of closet. I tear open the door to find this room is mostly empty, save a few couples making out on couches. They barely look up as I dart for a far window and flick the lock open, shoving up with my arms as I hear the stampede closing in beyond the far door.

"There she is!"

The glass hits its limit and I'm ducking under it and flinging myself the four feet or so to the garden bed outside before they can reach me.

I...don't know where to go. There's nothing really around here for miles. It's why kids like the Stackman House so much for parties.

And I can't go to the main road naked. I just...can't. The thought of being seen like this by more people is horrifying.

But there's no time to hesitate.

I hear a door yank open on creaky, rusted hinges and the second and third worst voices in the world speak in rapid succession.

"Find her," Blake says. "But save her for me."

"On it," Mike echoes.

My feet slip in mud, but my hands dig in and pull me forward until traction takes and I'm running into the woods faster than I've ever run before. Rain lashes my back until I reach the treeline, where it's only a little better. In here, it's a shower rather than a full storm, but it's cold. I'm cold, and shivering from more than lack of clothes.

I feel undone. Lost. Uncertain. Scared. Where the fuck *do I go? And not just right now. This world is fucked. People are fucked.* I'm *fucked.*

In one fell swoop, and with no consideration whatsoever, Emily Deutch destroyed my life.

There's no going back to school, is there? If the rest of the school hasn't already seen the pictures, they'll hear the stories; it'd be like walking into Hell. But I can't stay home either—Mom doesn't like that I live there now. *Maybe I can drop out and get my GED? But then all the hard work I put into escaping this place will be wasted. It feels as if some cruel person saw me working on a jigsaw puzzle and hid the loose pieces before swiping what was already complete onto the floor.*

But she'll have to wait. I hear heavy breathing and duck into a bush, tumbling into narrow branches that bite. I keep my body as still as I can and wait until a dark figure appears. He pauses right where I'm hiding—I'm three feet from his legs, too scared to look and see which one of them found me.

"Ava!"

I slam my hand over my mouth to keep from whimpering. It's Red-Eyes. He's hunting me too! Which means Black-Eyes is probably out here somewhere.

Four. Four of them. How can I outrun four *of the largest men I've ever seen?*

"Ava please! Let me help you!"

Help *me? If he wanted to help me, he could have done it*

inside! Before *they tore my dignity away from me!*

He doesn't want to help. He wants to make it worse. They all do. They're all the same.

"Ava! Trust me please! I swear this just went wrong!"

So wrong it can't be fixed.

So wrong I'm crouched in the icy mud naked and bruised and terrified.

I'm actually relieved seconds later when he sprints away like a nightmare.

I wait until I can't hear his panting anymore and cut perpendicularly through the forest. Some part of me knows that running blindly into the woods is stupid, but lost is better than brutalized. I've kept myself alive on far less than berries and rain in the past; I can do it again if I must.

Gah, my heart is pounding *with every step I run. Sharp rocks slice into my feet, branches and leaves whip across my naked skin. The fact that I was so turned on moments before all of this started is messing with my mind, my body, my soul. Two of those three parts of myself are mistaking this for play...*

But it's not play. It's darkness and terror here. And it doesn't take too long to realize finding the road is literally my only real option of escape. I need someone with a car to take pity on me. Maybe I could flag down a female driver. Maybe she has somewhere I can go until I figure out what to do.

The thought of her, this imaginary person, stops me where I stand—and it's just in time. No sooner do I pause but I hear running water. Pouring *water. A waterfall.*

A cliff. I catch a glimpse of it two dozen feet ahead of me as lightning streaks the sky blue.

I wouldn't have seen it. I would have run right off the edge in the dark.

I inch closer until I realize what it is—it's the town's old quarry. On the other side, brightly lit windows peek out of the woods like fairy lights tempting me closer. It's the closest proper neighborhood to the Stackman House. Those windows might as well be lighthouses calling me to shore. I sail toward them on my feet, fueled by pure adrenaline.

I'm so focused on them, I don't notice the tall, wide shape bearing down on me. I don't see the sprinting darkness until it barrels into me so fast I literally spin over my own body.

I hit the muddy ground at a brutal angle, rattling me. The world goes out of focus for long enough, it feels unreal. Like the world is a dream I'm about to wake up from.

But it's only another nightmare.

Mike looms over me, catching his breath with a smile on his face as if this is some sort of proud achievement for him. For all I know, it is.

"Blake! I got her!" he shouts.

I roll onto my back to take the pressure off the shoulder that struck the ground first, but Mike's eyes light up even more as he rakes his slimy gaze down my bare body.

"Phew!" he whistles. "You know, the kids at school might call you fat, but it's in all the right places, girl. More cushion for the pushin'."

I blink away the daze as quickly as I can. I flex my fingers and toes to check that everything is okay enough to run. When I do, something hard and round catches under my hand—a stone! Mike doesn't notice as I curl my fingers around it.

He's too busy smiling at...Blake. Blake's eyes catch on me before he's even come to a halt; I try to curl my legs upward, to hide myself any little way I can—

"Aw, she thinks that'll do anything," he laughs. "Hold her down."

I hate that my first instinct is to freeze. It's the worst feeling in the world to feel like my own body is betraying me at the exact moment I need it most.

Even more when Mike laughs, "She's just laying there.

She must want it, dumb skank."

*"It's not like she could pull guys like us any other way,"
Blake says, reaching for his belt.*

"We can take turns. How do you want her first?"

"You choose, man," Mike says.

*Blake's voice hums with malice. "Eh, I'm a sucker for eye
contact."*

"Please don't," I beg.

*But Mike only laughs again, coming around to kneel
above my head. His knees pin my hair. His musk—vanilla
and orange—is like a stink cloud bearing down on me from
above, mixing with Blake's overpowering sage, making me
sick. Mike's muscled hands press down on my upper arms
and that disgustingly attractive face the girls at school ogle
so much is suddenly inches from my own, leering at me the
way a mean kid might leer at the beetle whose wings he's
pulling off.*

*And I hate him. I hate Mike more than I've hated anyone
in my life, short of Emily. Even though I know Blake is about
to outrank him, there's something about Mike's cowardice,
the groveling evil smile on his face that rolls my heart in
acid.*

In the end, though, it's his cruelty that saves me.

*It's something so small, something I've never experienced
that snaps me out of my helplessness.*

*Mike's head recoils only an inch. His lips purse suddenly
and then—*

*Hot, mucous-y spit splatters my cheek just below my left
eye.*

He spit on me.

He spit on me!

*And everything I was before—whoever Ava Dillard could
have been—blinks out of existence.*

*Someone else steps into her place. Hard to explain—it's
like an instantaneous software update inside me. It's like*

cocking a gun. It's like spinning a coin on a table and slamming your hand down on top of it.

I'd rather die, I decide. I'd rather fight until my last breath. I'd rather take him with me.

I throw my head upward, slamming it into his head so hard my vision fills with stars...I just power through it.

The stone's in my hand, rising.

Connecting with his worthless skull.

Then I sit up. Turn and strike him again.

There's red...just a trickle. Pfft, I've seen more in my underwear on a day when a pad fails me.

I expected him to fall backward, but he doesn't. On his knees, with his heels behind him, he folds toward me instead and I hit him again.

And again.

Until he gets the message.

Until he learns his lesson.

Until he STOPS. FUCKING. TOUCHING. ME.

When he finally rolls away, my brain registers the red-painted rock in my hand for half a second; it's all the time I get before someone slams it away—Blake.

"You crazy bitch!" he shouts right in my face.

So close I feel vibrations of his voice in the wetness of Mike's spit on my cheek.

And my rage swells again.

Punching. I'm punching his face, screaming, before he can pin me down.

My leg presses against my chest, and through my foot, I feel Blake's ribs, pressing. Then lower—the most sensitive part of him. The weapon he was about to use on me.

I rear back and kick as hard as I can, striking true. The giant coward falls back with a scream, clutching his balls.

Good. I hope he never gets the chance to use them. And if he does, I hope I sterilized the bastard.

I'm up and running before I can blink.

I tear through the forest like its newest nightmare creature come to life.

"Ava, wait!"

I don't know who that is. I don't care. Fuck every last one of them. If I never see any of them again, it'll be too soon.

CHAPTER 15

Emily staggers to her bare feet like a skittish newborn foal. She sort of is one, I suppose. Reborn in the afterbirth of the cruelty she bestowed so freely unto others. One of her hands cups her non-existent breasts. The other covers her crotch.

But it leaves her bum exposed and someone with a feather reaches out and tickles her ass, to scare her. She leaps three feet in the air, screeching for them to stop. This kicks off another round of laughter.

Not from Crimson and Shadow, though. They both step in front of me, almost blocking the scene out, forcing my attention to them.

"Beautiful smile," Shadow says.

"I didn't even realize I was," I admit.

"It's glorious, little witch. Exactly how we remember it," Crimson adds, before leaning forward and laying a kiss on my lips. The touch is so delicate, it feels like it belongs in a fairytale. Shadow is less subtle. He grips me and dips me back for a deep kiss before setting me on my feet again.

"After this last part with her," Shadow says, letting his hand roam dangerously close to that little hidden toy still tucked inside me, "you'll stay with me. It's my turn to worship your ass in private."

I shiver at the words. "Okay."

But a soft frown plays at Crimson's mouth. The creases

at the center of his brow suggest worry, concern as he asks, "Have you had enough revenge yet?"

Have I? I honestly don't know. I feel lighter than I ever have before in my entire life. But is this enough for what I went through?

Crimson seems to be wondering the same. "It doesn't have to end now. We—" He motions to himself and Shadow "—are prepared to go further with you."

My brow quirks at that. "What does that mean?"

Some unspoken argument passes between them.

"We know what you went through that night," Shadow says.

A second later, Crimson echoes, "We read what you wrote about that night. We know what happened in the woods. She deserves worse than to be humiliated."

I gulp. I…told The Company everything up until the point I attacked Mike. I only used euphemisms then—that I pushed him off and ran. But they know what Blake was prepared to do to me. They know how scared I was as I ran away from him, terrified he would hunt me down and rape me right there in the mud.

My back tightens as I wonder at the meaning of Crimson's statement.

I really hope he's not offering what I think he's offering.

Jealousy and heartache flare in me at the suggestion. I don't want my Crimson and Shadow tainted that way. But more than that, what comes after we're done with her belongs to *me*—I refuse to let her ruin it OR steal it from me. Punishing Emily is my hearty, nutritious meal, what comes after is my dessert.

"Are you offering to…hurt her…the way *I* was almost hurt?" I ask.

"No!" Shadow practically leaps forward as the word leaves his mouth. "We wouldn't touch her in a thousand years. Not like that."

"Good, okay." Relief blows out of me as I grab their hands and cling. "She can't have you."

I hate to sound so pathetic, but…this is *my* fantasy. Just the thought of her getting to experience any part of them makes me want to be done with her *immediately*. If that's the only other option for revenge I have, then I'm done with revenge.

"*Fuck her*…b-but not literally," I almost beg. "You're mine. Only mine tonight."

Strong arms envelop me in our little triangle, blotting out the rest of the world as they step closer. Warm, reassuring kisses rain down across my head, my temples, my shoulders.

"Of course we're yours, little witch," Crimson growls.

"And you're ours. Don't you forget it," Shadow adds.

The words cradle me, caress me—I *definitely* need way more therapy than I think I do. Yikes.

"We only meant," Shadow says after a moment. "She doesn't have to walk away from this. We can end her for you tonight."

I blink, thinking I must have misheard him. "Do you mean you'd kill her?"

Crimson nods, and in a voice of stone promise, he says, "Grave's already dug, baby. One word from you and she's dead."

CHAPTER 16

TEN YEARS EARLIER

"Please! Please open the door!"

I'm pounding on the first door I come to, but nobody's answering. So I run to the next house. A dog barks viciously before I can even ring the bell, so I run for the next.

"Hello? Anybody, please!"

I pound on the door until my wrist hurts. But...a light flicks on inside and it's the most beautiful thing I've ever seen. There's a porch swing with a cushion on it. Carefully, I pull the cushion off and wrap it across my naked body.

After a second, a middle-aged blonde woman answers the door, cigarette dangling from her smeared red lips.

"What-What-What?" she groans when she opens the door. Then she gets a look at me and her eyes narrow. "What do you want?"

What a question. Nothing I can really have. I can't call my mom; she'd never come. I can't call the police—Emily's dad is the sheriff. What are my options?

"P-Please, I was attacked," I say. "Up at the Stackman House. Do you have any—"

But she doesn't even let me finish my request, "I know all about what goes on up there. Little unfair to say you were attacked just because you let some boy use you."

I bristle. "Excuse me?"

"Young girls used to know better than to toss around accusations like that. Too many of our boys getting strung

up for trustin' the wrong girl."

I feel a coiling in my gut—the new darker version of me wants so badly to lash out, it's all I want to do.

Until she adds, "If you're not careful, you're gonna end up just like your mother, Ms. Dillard. That's not a good look on anybody."

I don't know how this woman knows me. I don't care either.

"I just need clothes," I say, keeping my voice steady. "Please."

She sneers at the cushion across my body and disappears deeper into the house for a moment. I hear something move, a box maybe. Then she reappears with a large black shirt. She tosses it at me like touching me would make her unclean.

I turn it around to find it's a t-shirt for a church retreat from three years ago.

"Our pastor might be able to help you out if you're ready to be a better sort of girl," she says, reaching for the doorknob. "Put that cushion back before you leave. I'd hate to have to tell the sheriff you were stealing."

The door shuts in my face, robbing me of the little warmth I could feel pouring out of her house.

I leave her cushion half in and out of the rain as I walk away. Turning the shirt inside out, I force it over my head, relieved at least that it reaches my thighs even though it only takes a few feet for the rain to soak it through.

It doesn't matter.

If I didn't know my time in this town was done when Emily attacked me...or when I attacked Mike...it is now.

And I have to leave before anybody knows what happened in those woods. If Mike's hurt...or dead...my life is over. No one would ever believe what happened up there if I told them, especially not with Emily and her dad involved. It's too easy to write it all off on me.

So, I follow my feet home. Even from outside, I can

already hear my mom howling like a cat in heat, screwing some guy in the living room, but I can't be bothered to give a shit anymore. I'm never going to see her after tonight anyway.

I thrust open the front door and march up the stairs before either gross naked body can register my arrival.

"You got a kid?" the guy asks.

"Just a roommate," Mom says.

I roll my eyes and race to my room, slamming the door behind me. I change into the first comfortable clean clothes I find—ones so loose they don't touch me too much. I grab a backpack, my wallet, the money I've hidden under the floorboards. Any little thing I can't live without—there aren't many of those. I'm suddenly grateful everything I love can fit in a backpack.

"Ava? I told you not to come home!" She pounds on the door when she realizes it's locked. "What the hell did I say about locked doors in my house?"

I shove my feet in a pair of sandals—the only other pair of shoes I have aside from the sneakers they tore off my body.

Then I unlock the door. "I'm going," I tell her before she can speak.

But she doesn't like that. She follows me to the bathroom. "You take your attitude somewhere else, all right? I do too much for you to act like a spoiled bitch all the time."

"Well, you won't have to worry about that anymore," I say, shoving my tooth and hairbrushes into the bag. I take a bar of soap from the cabinet too, just in case I don't find a place to shower soon.

"What does that mean?"

I don't answer. I just move past her down the hall to the stairs, down to the kitchen. If she thinks I'm leaving her with all the groceries I just bought, she's got another thing coming.

"Ava! What the hell does that mean?"

"It means your 'roommate' is moving out. Go live the life you always wanted."

I shove sandwich bread into my backpack beside my hoodie, then the new jar of peanut butter in the cabinet. I wish I could take the jam I bought, but she's already made a mess of the jar.

"Yeah right. I'll see you tomorrow," she sneers...until I go to leave the room and she steps in my way.

"Move," I tell her.

"Lose the attitude, kid. It's boring."

"Move please." But she doesn't; she only rakes her gaze down my body looking for something to criticize. And I can't take her awful fucking judgment. I shove past her a little too hard; she hits the wall with a surprised yelp.

I ignore the pang of guilt I feel. It wouldn't have happened if she had just moved!

"You dumb bitch," I hear Mom say. "You apologize to me. Right now, or don't bother coming back."

She really doesn't get it. I almost feel sorry for her.

Almost.

But hand on the doorknob, I turn back anyway. "Mom, I'm sorry. Just remember, as awful as you are, I don't hate you."

Her sneer disappears as her face contorts with some other emotion I'm not sticking around to interpret. I'm out the door and around the far street corner by the time she bothers to scream my name.

CHAPTER 17

Crimson and Shadow's offer to end Emily Deutch's life for me hangs in the air between us.

"Is that...allowed?" I ask. "I don't want to go to jail because of her."

Crimson's smirk is dark and proud. "Jail doesn't exist for people like us."

I blink, absorbing his words. In a way, he's right. White-collar criminals are harder to pin down. Most get caught for tax evasion or embezzlement. Even when they *are* found guilty, their prisons are basically less boujee rehabilitation centers. But...murder's on another level.

"The Company takes care of its clients," Crimson clarifies.

Oh.

I suddenly understand why their fantasies cost as much as a down payment on a mansion. Or maybe they have judges in their pockets. Politicians. District Attorneys. I mean, Lucy, the partner at my firm who told me about them, probably represents clients for them. Maybe I'll be expected to too.

Crimson and Shadow part to reveal Emily is on her knees again, scooping up bits of her dress to hold against herself while more guests attempt to tickle or prod or flick their fingers at her. Tiny touches, scary in their unpredictability. Every time their finger lands on her shoulder or her head, she flinches away crying.

But it's the way she flinches when people suddenly pull cell phones from their clothing and begin to take pictures of her that tells me what I need to know. Even if she never feels bad about what she did to me all those years ago, she'll carry this night with her for a long time. She'll be tormented by paranoia, wondering if those photos will ever end up on some revenge porn website, or sold to perverts, the same way I worried about it for years after that night at the Stackman House when she stripped my dignity from me.

Besides, killing her would mean I'd have to drag the memory of her into my future with me. No thank you. She doesn't deserve one iota of my attention after tonight.

"No. I want her to live with it," I say finally. "Let's make her fear for her life but let her go. I want to forget she ever existed."

Shadow nods reverently, as if making some unspoken vow.

"Thy will be done, little witch." Crimson slides his hand into my hair and pulls me in for another long passionate kiss, leaving me breathless. Then he teases, "The next time you see me...remember to run."

Then they turn away and prowl closer to Emily, like jaguars stalking prey. Sky circles her with them.

"I can't believe you brought this bitch to our party," Crimson says, beginning the play.

"Man, I'm sorry," Sky says. "I never thought she'd act this way."

"This fucking slut insulted our girl," Shadow says. His voice is a purr, but not one of pleasure, only of warning. "I think we ought to teach this worthless whore a lesson."

"Fuck you!" Emily still manages to scream...and some small part of me admires her for it. I mean, isn't that what I did to Mike? I refused to take his abuse lying down.

Crimson ignores her. He talks over her at Sky. "What's

she like?"

"What do you mean?"

"Is her cunt as uptight as the rest of her?"

Sky smirks. "The pussy's pretty good for a village bicycle. Everyone's had a ride, but it *was* a damn good ride."

If Emily's mean eyes could slice him in half, he'd be in pieces on the floor. Rich, considering it's what she called me. In fact, all the insults we've hurled at her tonight have come directly from the details I gave them. They are things she or the others said to me at the Stackman House. She doesn't remember that; I can tell from the indignation on her face. She doesn't remember a single thing she said to me. She ruined my life and never lost a minute of sleep over it.

But that was always her problem. Even though she can't take it, she could always dish it out. And that is why she's here tonight—that's the *beauty* of tonight. If she hadn't transgressed, I wouldn't have punished her. She just couldn't help herself, not back then and not now.

And so the play continues.

The room sort of pauses as she pushes herself up off the floor to stand again. There's no telling what she's going to do, but the path to the front door has been intentionally left open. It's a narrow path through a party of people fully ready to make her escape difficult, but it's there and she can see it just past Sky.

For a second, I think she's going to take it, but then she growls and launches herself at Sky instead, claws extended like she was caught mid-transformation into a banshee.

He doesn't seem surprised. He bats her hands away with a laugh and turns her in the same movement, capturing her in his arms.

"You got her?" Crimson asks.

"Yeah, I got her."

"Let me go!"

"Come on, there's a room down the hall we can use,"

Crimson says, raising his voice to the party to add, "We can all take turns on her. Does that sound fun?"

Like the screech of the damned, the entire room roars to life with noise and cheers, and Emily begins to weep. Her little shoulders sag as tears streak her mascara down her cheeks.

"Who says I don't throw the best parties," Crimson teases in quiet triumph.

"Hell, this is the only way she could pull guys like us anyway," Shadow adds.

"I call first dibs," Sky declares.

"How do you want her first?" Shadow asks.

Sky squeezes Emily's cheeks with his enormous fingers, forcing her to look at him as he says, "Eh, it doesn't matter. I'm a sucker for eye contact."

And it's my turn.

"No," I call out. "Let her go."

"What?" Shadow barks, putting on one hell of a show of shrugging in disbelief.

It's so convincing, even Emily looks up at me.

"But baby," Crimson pouts.

I ignore my body's visceral reaction to the pet name *baby* again, knowing I'll get to hear it again soon enough.

"I think she's learned her lesson," I say. "And if she hasn't, God have mercy on her soul."

With that, Sky lets go of her completely, sort of shoving her lightly away from him. But Shadow is there hemming her in again. His hand snaps out and takes hold of her jaw.

"Say thank you," he says.

"What?" Emily's voice skitters, as thin as ice.

"She just saved you," Shadow repeats, nodding at me. "Say thank you."

"That's not necessary," I play it up.

"It is to me, baby," Crimson says, darting forward a little, to spook her. "Say it."

"No!" she barks.

Crimson's lips part in disdain and genuine surprise. "You can't even say thank you? You really *are* a piece of work."

"Do you have *any* idea who I am?" Emily yanks out of Shadow's grasp. "Do you have any idea what I'm going to do to you tomorrow?" Her eyes are little blue sapphires of rage as they snap to me. "I'm going to make your life a living hell, bitch."

In this moment, I honestly feel sorry for her. Sorry...and vindicated.

Not being saved that night ten years ago taught me a lot— the general unfairness of the world, the fact that fate is a lie used to keep people passive, that my own life was entirely mine to save or lose. It forced my hand in ways I never imagined. It showed me what I was capable of. But that doesn't mean I wouldn't have taken every scrap of help if anyone had offered.

I can only wince at her. "You do understand I could change my mind right now, right? With a snap of my fingers, you don't exist anymore."

Her face falls. She seems to remember she's surrounded. The fact that she *could* forget...the entitlement. It's a level of delusional self-confidence that would absolutely inspire a less enlightened version of me to snap my fingers.

I won't. Even with everything that's happened tonight, I'm still the bigger person here. Doesn't mean I can't punish her for being so small, though.

"All right, have at her, I guess," I say, waving the whole mess away.

She doesn't move and I feel sorry for her again, recognizing the same instinct in her to freeze, like I did. But Sky seems prepared for that. He splays his massive fingers wide and slams his open palm in between her shoulder blades, to knock her out of her daze...and she's moving. Sprinting. *Dodging.*

"Get her!" someone across the room shouts, echoed by someone else, "Save a piece for me!"

But they only fake reach for her, letting their hands slide across her body in passing as she screams and runs and pulls away from them.

When she disappears into the hall, Crimson loudly declares, "Let's get her!"

And a wave of guests swells for the door, led by Sky and Crimson. I hear Emily's screams grow louder and louder before a door opens, thunder crashes, and her voice fades away as she runs out into the storm.

The noise rises, crests, and then crashes to nothing as the entire party charges after her into the night. It goes from chaos to almost total silence, save for the rain. The band has remained in the room, but other than them, the only person still here with me is Shadow.

He turns to me with a megawatt smile on his face—and some bittersweet déjà vu hits me. It's a smile that feels familiar, inviting. It's...a lovely sight. He runs to me and picks me up, swinging me around, just as the band begins a song not meant for dancing. It's almost atmospheric, background sound you'd hear in a movie. Quiet and moody.

When Shadow sets me on my feet again, he slides my hands into position on his body to slow dance, even though it doesn't match the music.

"That was *so fucking hot!*" he declares, planting a kiss on my brow that I can feel all the way in my tailbone...and the toy jostling inside me as we move.

"Thank you," I tell him, just in case it needs to be said. "For helping tonight. Nobody ever cared back then."

He slows us to a gentle stop, studying me. His beautiful smile folds into a soft frown.

"I just mean...I didn't tell The Company everything that happened to me after that party, how hard it was on my own. I thought my life was over. I left town while I still could, with a backpack full of stuff to help me start again in another state" —I catch myself trying to monologue on him— "Whoa. Sorry, I shouldn't be dumping all of this on you."

"It's all right."

"No, it's too much."

"You are *not* and have *never* been too much." His giant, warm hand leaps to cup my cheek as he says, "I want to know what happened."

A spiked ball of tension stabs at the back of my dry throat. I don't know if I'm supposed to share this stuff, or if he even really cares, but...when am I ever going to have another chance to tell anyone about it? I hate to turn him into a confessional but I think he understands I need this.

"Are you sure?"

His nod is a lovely, sure thing. A green light I've been waiting a decade for.

CHAPTER 18

TEN YEARS EARLIER

I thought I knew what it felt like to be alone, but it was all just preparation for this. I'm sitting on the bus stop bench waiting for the 5:04 bus out of town with a backpack at my feet, clutching my cell phone in my hand and ignoring every call and text my mom tries to send.

None of them say nice things, but I keep hoping she'll just ask me to come home.

She doesn't. Every text is just some new revelation of something that pisses her off about me. Every text is one more nail in the coffin of any relationship we could ever have.

Especially once the lifestyle texts start rolling in. The guilt trips about 'who's going to pay half my rent?' 'I work twelve hours shifts to support you, making dinner is the least you can do.' 'If you think I'm going to keep your room the way it is for you, you've got another thing coming.'

That's what she's really sad about losing—someone to blame for all her problems. Not me.

By the time the bus finally pulls up and I climb aboard and claim a seat, she destroys what's left of our relationship for good. My heart was already cracking from everything else I endured tonight, but when she texts me 'If I had known what an ungrateful child I'd have, I would've aborted you,' my heart shatters completely. The bits of glass rain down through my soul, slicing and cutting in ways I know will eventually cause scar tissue to form. I'll never be the same regardless of whether I can heal myself or not.

And I don't just mean emotionally.

When I'd initially arrived at the bus stop, I'd visited the bathroom to give myself a sink-shower and found a cut on my leg almost six inches long. It wasn't bleeding anymore, but...it bothers me that I can't tell if it was from someone clawing at me, or falling through the hole in the stairs, or climbing through the window, or crawling into the bush to hide, or getting tackled off my feet by Mike.

It bothers me that there are so many ways in which people hurt me tonight.

The sting becomes my only companion on the six-hour bus ride. The only one I trust anyway, past the men who keep leering at me and whispering gross things under their breath. It keeps me focused. I spend the entire trip writing out a list of responsibilities nobody's going to help me with moving forward on a scrap piece of paper.

But after that's done, worse and pressing problems bully their way into my brain.

How long will it take them to connect me to Mike's injuries? Blake would surely tell them, right? Will I have to flee the country? Can I even do that?

What happens when video and photos of what they did to me at that party get out? What if someone uses them against me later?

I can't sleep a wink the entire trip to the city.

And then I'm denied sleep again when I get to the cheapest hotel I can find, only to have the skeevy guy behind the desk tell me he can "give me a room" if I'm willing to "show him what my mouth can do." He then refuses me a room entirely when I tell him I hope his dick rots off.

I mean, what did he expect me to say?

The next place is only a little better, but...I lock both door locks and wedge a chair under the handle when I get inside.

Then I spend the entire day glued to the television, waiting for any sort of news story about Mike. Surely there would be something.

But there isn't. Not the first day, or the second either.

On the third, I find the nearest library and stalk the social media of everyone at my school who might have been at that party, looking for any news.

When I find it, though, I don't really know what to say other than that the news is wrong. Wrong in a big way.

There's only one story in the local paper...and the headline reads: **Tragic Accident at Stackman House Claims Lives of Two Teens During Thunderstorm**

Two teenagers lost their lives late Friday night in a tragic accident at the Ohlie Quarry during a severe thunderstorm. Authorities report that the victims, Blake Sturgess and Mike Bauer, both athletes at Greenfield High, accidentally fell off a cliff while attending an unsanctioned party at the derelict Stackman House.

According to the Greenfield Police Department, nearly five hundred teens were at the gathering when the storm hit. Witnesses stated that the party was already chaotic, with numerous young people drinking and taking risks as the storm worsened.

"Blake and Michael appear to have walked too close to the edge of the cliff without realizing how slippery and dangerous the terrain was. They were found about 30 feet below the ledge," Sheriff Jeffrey Deutch of the Greenfield

Police Department said.

Although friends and girlfriends of both young men were at the party, they said they didn't realize either was missing until near dawn. Emergency responders arrived shortly after the 911 call came in around 6:45 AM, but by the time they reached the scene, both teens had already succumbed to their injuries. Officials confirmed that both victims suffered severe neck and head trauma attributed to the fall and were later found submerged in the quarry's waters.

The incident is believed to have been accidental, with alcohol being a likely contributing factor...

I don't know what to make of it. I genuinely don't. I'm not even sure I believe it. It seems too lucky. Too kind after everything.

And that's what it must be—a trick. The world has never been kind to me. That night gave me a lifetime worth of proof.

Besides, this was Emily's boyfriend. *I wouldn't believe for a second she didn't run to her daddy immediately to find Blake when he didn't come back to the party. That's just— ha! No way.*

The only safe thing to do is to assume this is a trick. Some sort of cop mind game meant to make me let down my guard or come home where they're waiting to take me into custody.

I can't go back either way.

But that leaves me in an unsafe, unfamiliar city with no safety net to cling to. When I leave the library and return to the hotel, some creep whistles at me and follows me into the lobby. I "sleep" with the chair under the knob again and it's the only reason the door stays closed in the middle of the night when a man scratches at the knob, bangs, and kicks until he gets frustrated and leaves. I'm too scared to get close to the door to peek through the peephole. Halfway to calling the cops, I realize I can't. All I can do is wait until dawn like a reverse vampire and flee.

The next day, I find a women's shelter with an opening and move in there.

But I have to leave again the second they ask me my age, then demand to see my ID, and I'm too scared to give it. Too scared they'll send me home.

It sucks. The nonsense between me and a safe night's sleep is horrifying. I try another hotel, but it's nicer and they demand ID too. I try a homeless shelter, but it's full. I try an all-night diner but the man behind the counter refuses to let me stay even though I'm buying food. It's like he can tell I need the shelter...and hates me for it.

It's another week of moving around, narrowly finding places to sleep before a guy with a knife pulls me into an alley and steals the little money I have left. After that, I carry a face-breaking stone around in my pocket, figuring if it worked once it can work again. I slowly lose all the feeling I ever had around being violent.

I come to accept that violence isn't the answer, but sometimes it's the only answer left.

Panhandling gets me enough to afford a gym membership for a month, so I can shower. I eat out of dumpsters to save the rest I make, hoping maybe I can save enough to afford that second-worst hotel again.

And I find myself crying more and more until there are no tears left and I shake a lot and my hoody gets a hole in it and the cold seeps in at odd times to warn me winter's almost here.

In the end, it's pure random luck that saves me.

While trying to find jobs that don't require IDs online at the library, I stumble upon a posting for a dog sitting job. A nice middle-class-looking couple are going out of town for four weeks and need someone to watch their doodle. It comes with cash, food in the fridge, and a bed—practically paradise.

I create a phony new social media page for 'Ava St. Jude' and walk around the city taking stupid smiling pictures of myself, changing my shirt and hairstyles a couple times so it looks like they were taken at different times. I approach every person I see with a dog and pretend to be in love with them so they'll let me take a picture petting them.

I let myself become 'the dog girl.'

Emily called me a bitch, so it feels appropriate to be saved by them. My people. My new four-legged friends.

Then I send a link to my profile to the couple, along with a letter and 'references,' which are just the numbers of women I met in the women's shelter who offered kindness to me before I was kicked out.

And I get the job. While eating a soggy waffle out of the dumpster behind a breakfast place, I get a text asking me to come for an interview. I go to the gym and take a shower, then I stuff my pockets with bacon and go to meet my new best four-legged friend.

Wouldn't you know it? 'Ducky the Doodle' loves me. And the couple are embarrassed to have to 'pay me in cash.' But they promise there's plenty of food in the fridge and freezer, money for more if I need it, and a friggen *hot tub in the back yard. All they ask is that I don't bring anyone over—and I assure them, they don't have to worry about that while leaving off the truth that there is no one to invite.*

I use every last second of that month to fix my pathetic life. I apply for more jobs—house sitting, dog sitting, tutoring. Anything that pays under the table. I double dip for a week when their neighbor strikes up a conversation and asks me to water her plants while she's away, which leads to a tutoring position with a family down the street...and another dog sitting job.

It takes almost six months of hobo-ing my way between stranger's guest rooms and couches to save enough for a quality fake ID and new social security number, erasing underage Ava Dillard and replacing her with newly 18-year-old Ava St. Jude.

Then, it takes a few more weeks to graduate from high school once I can pay to have my records forged too so I can take final exams. I don't feel too bad about that one; after all, they're the grades I actually earned, it's only the name that's different.

Unfortunately, finally getting back on track doesn't erase the memory of that night, or those people, or the strange disconnect I feel any time the memory of Mike's broken face robs me of sleep.

Or the fact that some of the kids at my old school still post about 'the night I disappeared.' Some of them think I fell in the quarry with Blake and Mike and my body just hasn't been found yet. Others say I pushed them.

I start a savings account at the bank and put away pennies each month until I have enough for a flight out of the country if I need one.

Blake's death isn't my business, but Mike is my fault. When I finally find a studio apartment that doesn't run a background check, it comes with a big ole clawfoot tub where I like to sit when it rains and the emotions get too crushing and the world seems like it's closing in. 'Tubby time' is about all the therapy I can afford, but it's enough to get me through the worst nights.

There is no cure for the paranoia, though. It haunts me worse than the rest. The belief that my life has already ended, I just haven't realized it yet; I feel like a ghost who doesn't know they're dead. Every decision I make—from college to taking the bar exam to taking high profile cases— is marred and distorted by the fear that I'll be recognized and destroyed all because of a bit of spit and a rock.

Everything about me is a muted version of what I could be.

Including my relationships. Especially *those. I don't deserve the good guys. The bad guys are reminders of what I never want to experience again. And either way, how am I supposed to actually trust anyone?*

Eventually, though, a need deeper than my fear creeps into my life—the need for revenge. The need to take my power back. The need to make *Emily feel what I felt.*

But tied to that is a darker desire that scares me as much as it thrills me.

I want to be chased.

Hunted.

Taken.

For the right *reasons, this time.*

What are the right reasons? It's hard to qualify them. I only know that there's a version of that night at the Stackman House where Red-Eyes and Black-Eyes chased me to exhaustion. Maybe even one where Blake really wanted me too.

And once I let that vision escape the dark corner of my mind where it was hiding, there's no other fantasy that will cut it. I try "self-medicating" with different types of porn, trying to find some solution to this growing dark hunger in me to be desired so badly. I even try telling my therapist about the fantasy. She has theories about it—plenty of theories—but they all revolve around that night *and the unfinished business of it.*

And the desire to be hunted never goes away. It only grows more fiery, more desperate, more explicit. It goes from a simple chase in my mind to an entire erotic stage play with multiple acts. It's like watching a movie in my head, one where I can twist and reorder the plot points for each pleasure session so the fantasy never grows stale.

At one point, I contact my old high school and buy a yearbook for the year I was supposed to graduate. I spend literal days going through every male student's picture until I eliminate all the unlikely candidates for Red-Eyes and Black-Eyes—the jocks, the nerds, the theater kids—and land on a dozen possibilities.

I even create a fake profile on a dating app to match with them, but I struggle with it. There always comes a point where I ask them if they were at that Stackman party, and when they say yes, a cold chill runs through me wondering if they were one of the people who stripped me. If they were one of the ones who took pictures of me. And hate trickles into me as hot as molten steel, making it almost impossible to continue flirting with them, even to get the information I want.

It's unhealthy, I realize. For me.

I can't keep reimagining the past. It just leaves me feeling forsaken.

For a little while, I'm able to lay the revenge fantasy to rest.

But the sexual fantasy persists.

The fantasy of Red-Eyes, Black-Eyes, and Blake all chasing me because they really want me *haunts every twisted waking moment of my life...and all the nights too.*

Until finally...like a gift from the universe...I go out for drinks with a partner who works at my law firm. Lucy's a party girl, and it doesn't take long for 'a few drinks' to become a bender, during which she lets slip that there's a company that specializes in fulfilling fantasies. Even ones as complex as mine.

And I find myself wondering if it's time to reclaim the worst night of my life...

CHAPTER 19

When I reach the end of my story, I have no expectation of the reaction I'll get from Shadow, but he still surprises me. He grimaces and his dark eyes narrow with…empathy, I think? He looks distraught. A little trapped. Uncertain.

None of the things I wanted to inspire in him before the grand finale of my fantasy begins.

"Fuck, forget I said anything," I beg him, glancing away, absolutely mortified by my own awkwardness. Leave it to me to make the *escort* uncomfortable. Ha!

"No, wait," he says. "Thank you for sharing that heavy shit with me."

"Yeah, it's…sorry."

"Ava."

"Sorry, I'm fine, really."

"Ava, look at me."

He ducks a little trying to get me to meet his gaze, but I can't quite raise my head to do it. When I can't, he…well…tries to "help" me. It's the strangest thing. His long, strong fingers snake into my hair and fist, not to pain, but with passion, and he uses the grip to force me to look up at him. When I meet his gaze, I'm met with more fire than I expected. More pain. More desire. More sincerity than I was prepared for.

"Goddesses don't apologize, you hear me?" he growls. "Our girl doesn't apologize. The woman who just crushed her enemy into the dirt doesn't apologize."

Right—he's trying to get me back into character. I take a deep breath and shake the embarrassment away.

"Of course," I try, even though it sounds foreign on my tongue. "Blah, I'm being silly."

"No, you're being real," he counters. "You survived things you never should have had to. If anyone should apologize, it's us. It's our fault we didn't find you in time that night. You have *no idea* how much we've punished ourselves for it. But the past is dead now. We're your present. We're your future. He and I have had ten years to think about how different life will be for all of us now that we're together again. And sweetheart? It's just getting good, all right? It will only ever get better now. You have my word."

Gah, did he just come up with that on the spot? Honestly, does it matter? It's exactly the sort of declaration I've wanted to hear my whole life—the sort of promise that has the potential to erase decades of meanness. I don't even care that it's made up. It puts a smile on my face that could light up the night sky.

His eyes dart to my smile with hunger and that brightens my smile even more.

I untwine his hand from my hair and tug him to follow as I say, "Come on, let's go get this thing outta my butt so we can have fun."

No more sad mopey stuff; that's not what he's getting paid to deal with. He's getting paid to make me feel desired, and with that in mind, I pull him into a downstairs bathroom, lock the door, and wrap my arms around his neck all in the same motion, nearly toppling us both over.

"Whoa," he laughs. "Careful, sweetheart."

Sweetheart, I can deal with. On tiptoe, I curl my hand around the nape of his tattooed neck and pull him in for a deep kiss I can feel all the way in my diaphragm, especially when he slides his arms around my waist and tugs me tight against his broad chest. He backs us into something, slides his hands under my ass and lifts me, spinning us both so I'm the one pressed against the wall.

Fuck, it's dizzying. Like lightning through the center of me.

Then it's all lips and tongues and teeth. A nip of my bottom lip, a trail of kisses along my jaw, pattered caresses along the column of my neck…all while his hands cup my ass…and at least one of his fingers lands on the rose plug handle sticking out of me. He wiggles it, scattering shivers. And when a tiny moan escapes me, I watch in real-time as the hairs on the back of his neck rise in response.

This is more like it.

"God, don't stop," I whisper.

He chuckles. "There's no chance of that tonight, sweetheart. No safe words either."

I shiver again, at the thought. He's right. No safe words. This is it. This is my chase.

The thought empowers me. Emboldens me. I pull his lips to mine, desperate for his taste, his soft tongue, his teasing kisses. I can't get enough. And I realize…I don't have to. This need, this *hunger* so long unsated, is its own animal tonight. There's no need to leash it here, with them. They're my safe space. They're my freedom to be every fantasy I've kept secret.

The thought cascades through my body triggering floodgates that squeak open on rusted hinges and tear loose of their welding. If there are no safe words, then there's no stopping what's about to happen, which means I don't need to worry about filtering my thoughts anymore.

"Baby?" I whisper at him.

He purrs against my lips, "God, call me that again."

"Baby." I tease his lips with the tip of my tongue. "I want you to take this thing out of me and replace it with something better."

He lets out a low dark chuckle. "You're in for a long night, you know. *Ten years* of us. Are you sure you want it to start now?"

Is he nuts? "Of course, I want it to start now! I want every last minute I can get—"

He doesn't even wait until I'm finished. He lowers me to my feet and fists my hair again, yanking this time, arching my back so fast my tits pop forward, brushing against him with each panted breath I take.

Eyes boring into my soul, he whispers, "Raise your dress."

I reach for it—

"Slowly," he snaps. Like this is a hostage negotiation. "That's it. So slowly."

I bunch the fabric in my hands and draw it up toward my hips as Shadow steps back to watch, never letting go of my hair. Soft as fingertips, like breath against my skin, I imagine his hands there, until the fabric passes the intimate place he and Crimson already explored in the car.

Fuck, just the memory makes me want his fingers there again so badly.

But his fingers want to be somewhere else.

He spins me to face the wall and tugs on my hair, pulling my head back until I can only peer up into his inky-black eyes as he pins himself to my back.

Staring into the depths of my soul, his free hand slides softly across my bum. But no sooner has his full palm made contact, then he rears back and whips his open palm across the peach hill of my ass. There's no pain, only impact and surprise…and an undeniable wetness pools between my legs.

He smacks my ass again and this time, there's just a tiny bite of pain and I gasp. He's watching me—my face—so closely for reaction that the second he knows he hurt me, his full hand lands on the spot, massaging-massaging the pain away. And his lips land against my forehead from above.

"Beautiful. *Beautiful!*" he whispers.

"What is?" I ask.

"The way your ass jiggles." His voice is breathless, heated. "I love the feel of it in my hand."

Even if I couldn't feel how hard his cock is against me—which I absolutely can—I'd know he means every word.

Especially when he groans, "That's where my hand belongs. You know that, don't you, sweetheart? One cheek for me, one for Crimson—we're both going to leave our mark tonight."

God. I tilt my head back a little more against his chest so my lips can reach his. Our mouths connect, but our tongues don't meet in fight and flurry. In this upside-down position, they slide across each other slowly, and our hums of satisfaction harmonize as thunder rumbles overhead.

Growling with anticipation, Shadow tears his lips away and presses his head to the back of mine and nudges me until my forehead's flat against the wall. His free hand slides across the peach of my ass again before it leaves me and I hear a drawer open.

"What are you—"

"Patience," he croons right before I hear the tiny *snick* of a bottle opening and warm lube drizzles down the gully just below my tailbone.

"You keep that stuff in all the bathrooms?" I joke.

"Tonight we do," he says. "Your chase is our pleasure. Ours is yours."

Suddenly, the plug is spinning inside me. Delicately at first, then quickly. It's such an odd, unexpected sensation, I giggle pressing myself a little tighter to the wall.

"You like that?" he asks.

"I've never felt that before," I admit.

"God, this fits you so well. I don't want to take it out. It's so beautiful."

I can't help but blush and turn my head a little. It's so intimate this moment, watching over my shoulder, spying on him as he plays with my body. But the look on his face—it's all the desire I've ever hoped to see.

Certain parts of my body clench and he notices in a big way. Maybe even feels it through his hold on the plug.

"*Fuck!* So much for patience."

Shadow lets go of my hair, but presses his lips to my cheek, pinning me, as he reaches around my hip and his fingers slide into place atop my swollen clit. He finds wetness there waiting for him and he growls again as he begins to move his fingerpads back and forth at a pressure just shy of feather brushed across skin. So soft, it honestly takes me off guard, especially as I feel his other hand take firm hold of the plug. The anticipation, the breath my body seems desperate to hold, and his warm, harried breath against my cheek—it overstimulates me in seconds. Ugh, I whimper. *I actually whimper!*

"God, you love this, don't you," he moans…right before there's a gentle tug and pressure as he coaxes the toy out of me. I whimper again.

I hear the toy land in the sink, discarded. I expect to hear a zip. I expect him to just take me. To ravish me, to raze who I was before and break ground on the newest version of Ava St. Jude.

But he doesn't.

He spins me again to face him and a streak of disappointment shoots through me at the exact moment a bright blue bolt of lightning streaks across the sky outside.

The lights flicker.

Then go out.

It's a moment of panting darkness where I wait for him to pounce.

But again, he doesn't. He pauses and glances away. Like

he's waiting for something.

A pale silver light flickers on outside. Just enough to light half the room, and half his face as he smiles at me.

"There we go," he says.

"What's that?" I ask.

"Ambiance. This is only stage one, sweetheart."

I feel another smile shoot across my face in anticipation, but I don't need any more foreplay to the foreplay.

I wrap my hand around his lapels and yank him in, tight and tighter against me. "Show me stage one, baby."

His smile is so radiant, it could cure blindness. "Your darkest wish is our command."

Again, I expect him to spin me…but he doesn't.

Instead, his hands slide down to his pants. I hear the button pop, the zip lower. And I know I'm only imagining it, but I *feel* the heat before I even look down and see the behemoth that pops forward to say hello to me.

My mouth waters at the sight of his glorious cock. How beautiful and engorged it is for me. I can't imagine there's much blood left in the rest of him. Hell, I can't imagine him *running* with that kickstand between his legs. But I can imagine plenty of other things.

With a confidence that almost bowls me over, he dips two fingers into my pussy, collecting some of my wetness and rubs it across his cock. Then he pushes down on the top so it's parallel to the floor before he presses the tip…to my thighs.

Thigh gap, thigh shmap. This wouldn't work if I had one.

He slides his cock between my full thighs slowly, letting his thick tip catch on my lips. Then he pulls it back, then in again, as we both watch. God, it's the strangest thing. It's nothing any man has ever done to me. Nothing any of them has ever wanted to do…but Shadow does. A groan escapes him like a prayer. No…like an *answered* prayer.

The feel of him.

He isn't even inside me yet, but it doesn't matter.

Intimate isn't a strong enough word for it. It's slow and deliberate and curious. Just for us. And it has my heart pounding so hard I can literally feel it in my pussy. If he makes me wait much longer, I'm going to fucking chase *him*, tackle *him*!

But he revels in my neediness. Delights in it.

"You know," he teases, "I never thought you'd let me catch you this easily."

I purse my lips playfully at him. "The chase hasn't even started yet."

"Exactly," he says, pushing between my thighs a little faster, before he pants, "You already know you belong to me."

My mouth opens to shoot off some snarky reply, but the words never make it. Shadow grips himself suddenly and shifts his angle, sliding up and inside me between my closed legs like a sword into the sheath specially made for it.

One moment I'm wet and throbbing and empty, the next I'm filled so deeply I'm pretty sure his cock reaches my brain and impales it clean through.

Then, he thrusts…and thrusts again!

"Holy fuck!" I don't say the words, I sort of bleat them in surprise over and over.

"It's not a holy fuck yet. That comes later."

I don't even know what that means. And it doesn't matter. His legs spread the tiniest bit so they can clamp around my thighs while he sheaths himself inside me again and again, fucking me. *Fucking me!*

Pinning me to the wall.

Growling against my skin.

Impaling me with a relentless force and pace that robs me of my poor excuses for fantasies—it's unreal. It's hallucinatory. It's all I've ever wanted. I lose myself in it—him—so fast, I already feel my body beginning to fracture with pleasure.

But…

But…!

He's so close. So imposing. So *consuming.* He's everything. Him and the sensation of him filling me so completely. Pinning me. Trapping me. His eyes bore into mine, unblinking—fixated to madness! He sees me! And he isn't afraid or turned off. The thought amplifies the pleasure—*god, the relentless mind-scrambling pleasure*—and sours it somehow.

For some reason, my hands are on his waist, trying to push him away *and* hold him close at the same time, and he's not indulging either extreme. He glances down at my hands mid-thrust…and chuckles.

"You can't escape this, Ava." Then he thrusts again and adds, "And you don't want to."

"I don't. I don't!"

"Fucking prove it to me."

I reach for the button-down under his suit. Fingers between buttons, I grip and yank, listening to the little things scatter across the tile floor as his shirt tears open, revealing his beautiful, sculpted chest underneath. It's dusted in fine blond hairs and scattered with more tattoos, although they're much softer than the ones at his neck.

All save one.

It takes me aback for a moment.

There, right at the center of his chest under his storm cloud tattoo collar, is a rose. But not just any rose. *My* rose. His is larger, almost the size of the actual flower, but it's the *exact* same tattoo that I have on my left shoulder—the one that looks like a simple outline but glows a brilliant neon pink under blacklight.

Identical.

Which wouldn't be a problem…except I never gave The Company details about my tattoo.

It wasn't relevant to the fantasy, so I said there was *a* tattoo, never a rose tattoo, and never this one specifically. And for a moment it feels like my heart is flash-freezing. Because it's not just the tattoo that's wrong.

"You called me Ava."

"Huh?" His rhythm studders.

"You called me Ava."

His brow furrows playfully. "That's your name."

The Company said my guys—my *actors,* my *escorts*—wouldn't be given my actual name; they would only refer to me as Little Witch, like Red-Eyes did ten years ago.

"But...you shouldn't know that."

Just like he shouldn't know about the tattoo.

Suddenly, the push and pull of my hands against him become all push. I shove him out of me so fast I almost fall flat on my ass. And the second we disconnect, the intimacy between us explodes into fear and panic and insecurity.

"I don't understand," I say, because I'm not sure what else *to* say. "Did you research me? Did you talk to somebody?"

Despite the raging thrumming demand of my pussy to *put that cock back where it belongs, so help me,* the entire bathroom feels cold. Claustrophobic. Unsafe. And I'm frozen. My body is frozen while my mind is racing a mile a minute inside me.

And he's not saying anything. He's frozen too. And I hate it. Every moment he just stands there, not saying anything, my mind is conjuring up the worst fucking possibilities imaginable. All while it veers violently away from *the dark reality* of why he has that tattoo and knows my name. It's as if my mind *can't stand* the thought of it, so it's skipping the obvious truth, searching for any other possible explanation.

"Say something!" I almost shout.

But what he says is bad. *It's bad!*

"Ava—"

"How the *fuck* do you know my name!"

"Because I'm—"

I cut him off and shove his chest. "Don't you *dare* lie about that! That is a *hard boundary* for me, okay?"

But he more than rebounds from the shove. He's suddenly against me, pressing me to the wall, looming over me with his hands on my cheeks and his face inches from mine, imploring me with raw sincerity in his eyes. I hate it!

"I'm not lying," he says. "I'd never lie to you. I'm—"

"You're not."

"Yes, I am, sweetheart. You called me Black-Eyes in your application to The Company, but my real name is—"

"No! You're not him," I say to convince myself. "You're some random good escort guy hired by The Company to pretend you're him. You went above and beyond with your character, that's all. A-And you figured out who I am, and "

"I saw you in Mr. Lawson's class," he says, dousing my system in ice water. "I saw you first, but Crimson saw you clearest. We went to every party that year waiting for you to show up, and you finally did and we failed you. I...I had so many chances to tell you how I felt about you and when you needed me most, fuck, I failed you."

Fight, flight, freeze. *Fight-flight-freeze!*

My mind cycles through my options, trying to decide. I can't seem to will my feet to move.

"Ava, I'm sorry. I am so—"

"Spit on me."

He freezes against me, in surprise, in confusion. Who cares!

"What?" he asks.

"If you're going to hurt me, I need you to spit on me so I can run, okay? Please."

Distress rolls across his face in waves. Distress and outrage. "Ava, I will chase you, hunt you, tie you down and fuck you—whatever you want—but I'll *never* spit on you the way Mike did. Not without a *long* fucking conversation first."

He says it so reassuringly…but it's anything but.

I told The Company about Mike, but only as much as I had to. For obvious reasons, I kept details to a minimum. I told them Mike and Blake chased me, tackled me, that I shoved them off, and escaped, but never what happened while I was pinned in the mud. I'd never incriminate myself like that. So there would be *no way* for Shadow to know Mike spit on me unless he was there. Unless he saw me get attacked *and did nothing to stop it!*

"This isn't funny anymore."

I shove past him for the door. He grabs for my wrist, but I pull away just as fast.

"Ava, wait."

"Fuck you for ruining this."

With that, I yank the door open and run.

CHAPTER 20

Without the crowds of guests clogging the hallways, it's a nearly straight shot to the front door, maybe forty feet away. I kick off my shoes as I bolt for it, imagining the path between me and the front gate, and how far down the road I saw the next house. I doubt they'll chase me that far; what would be the point? They're getting paid either way.

Hell, maybe I can ask the guy at the gatehouse to lend me his phone. It doesn't matter if he doesn't. I'm a runner. I can go any distance, especially if it means people don't play cruel jokes on me like this. Especially when I'm *fueled by pure rage* that the *experience I paid a small fortune for* was shot to shit like this. I'm not going to demand a refund, but they are getting three out of five stars from me *at best!*

God, it was *so good* before that asshole lost himself in his character. I don't care how he found out about the rose tattoo. I don't know how he found out about Mike. But fuck, it was just one step too far. Right? *Right?*

Or is this just another example of The Company's "attention to detail," as Lucy called it? Am I just ruining my own fantasy *again*?

I don't know. I don't know! I just wanted *the good versions* of Red-Eyes and Black-Eyes for one perfect night of terror. I just wanted the boogeymen to actually want me.

In the end, though, I'm a practical creature and I accept that it doesn't matter. *Anyone* who knows about what I did to Mike is dangerous.

With that, my hand lands on the front doorknob and I twist it open, taking the brunt of a warm, wet gust of stormy air as it rushes around me, enveloping me in the perfume of rotting petrichor and roses.

Then I freeze.

The entire front lawn is pitch black, save for the neon glowing blossoms…and a sudden blue bolt of lightning that shoots across the sky like a crack across a pane of glass. Movement catches my attention…and I see a flash of red, a human silhouette, before the lightning vanishes, plunging the garden into darkness once more.

"Has our chase begun, little witch?"

Crimson.

His voice carries out of the darkness, raising the hairs on my arms, crawling up my neck like a spider. I don't know if I should say anything about wanting to leave. About who Shadow claimed he was.

"Something wrong, little witch?"

His voice comes from a different direction this time, startling me. My head and heart leap ahead of me as I scour the darkness for signs of him. But there's only inky blackness until—

Lightning flashes again and he's there, barreling out of the darkness like a night terror.

I scream bloody murder. I wish I was cooler, but I'm not. I genuinely wasn't expecting him to charge at me…which is stupid, considering I came here for a chase.

I slam the door shut and turn to run, screeching to a cartoon halt the second I see Shadow *and* Sky blocking both exits to the grand foyer.

"Ava…"

Fuck! Just the sound of Shadow saying my name is worse than the spit; it lights a fire under my feet. I do the first thing that comes to mind—I race up the stairs like a damned bimbo in a horror movie! Stupid!

But I know this mansion has multiple staircases. And if all else fails, it has a thousand damned bedrooms and sheets I can turn into a rope and lower myself out a window.

I just have to keep moving. That's the important thing. Especially when I hit the second-floor landing and I hear the front door open.

Crimson almost hisses, "What are you two doing here? She wants us to chase her. Let's go! We can't fuck this up."

"She knows, C," I hear Shadow say…followed by a heavy silence I can feel in my bones.

I know I should run. I know I should use this time to gain distance, but my nosiness gets the best of me. I pause where I am in the shadows, listening.

"Fuck," Crimson says.

"What do you mean? What does she know?" Sky asks.

"No this is good," Crimson says instead of answering him.

"Good?" Shadow echoes.

"She *should* know," Crimson says. "It'll be better this way."

"*What does she know*?" Sky demands again. Again, he's ignored.

"She said the chase is off," Shadow says.

"*Nothing's* off," Crimson snaps back. "Get your head in the game. Give her what she *fucking* asked for. Give her everything. She deserves this."

There's only a moment of silence before music kicks in from somewhere—the band, maybe? Just like before Shadow took me in the bathroom, they're not playing a song, but a score. A score they clearly created for tonight. Its beat is dark and patient. It lurks in the air like some invisible pulsating beast, hunting. It spikes my heartrate immediately.

And then I hear it. It's so soft, I mistake it for rain until I realize what it really is—feet jogging up the stairs behind me. I spin just as Crimson steps onto the second-floor landing and pauses.

Our eyes connect; in the semi-darkness, he's somehow stepped into just the right spot for the silver light from outside to hit his eyes, brightening the orange in them. That, and the red of his mask remind me of only one person.

"Red-Eyes?" I ask him, hoping he won't play along.

"Yes?"

The simple answer delivered with such understated confidence stabs me with uncertainty.

"Tell me you're not him," I stammer. "Please."

"No can do, my little witch," he says, taking a step toward me.

I take a tentative step back. "Are you going to hurt me?"

Despite the mask, I can see his brow furrow deeply as he takes another step forward. "Never."

"But you said I d-deserve this."

"You deserve this and more. Everything you never had. Everything that was taken from you. Everything you've always desired. Including us."

I shake my head gently, backing away again. I *just can't tell* if this is theater or not. My heart is battering against the constraints of my ribcage with doubt.

"I want to leave, Crimson."

"You need *this*. You've been running scared for too long." He steps forward again, and this time I notice that his chest is...*heaving*. His body—his neck, his hands, his posture—is tense and rigid and when he speaks again, his voice pebbles with an anger so sharp it sounds as if it's cutting him. "You thrive in darkness, little witch. And I'm here to eviscerate the memory of that night for you. I'm here to replace that *loser* who couldn't reach you in time, that *failure* who couldn't stop those animals from touching you...with me."

A new type of confusion floods my system at his

declaration. Why would he be saying that if he was really Red-Eyes? More than that, why would his chest be heaving if he *wasn't*?

"Who are you really?" I ask one more time.

A beautiful sharp smile streaks across his face as his hands leap to his clothes…and tear. He sheds the top of his suit like a sanitarium patient shedding a straitjacket, and once it's gone, a rose tattoo at the center of his chest blooms in my awareness. It's the only tattoo on his beautiful body.

And it's suddenly inches from me as he closes the distance between us. The tattoo and his impossibly beautiful eyes with their rainbow colors.

He raises something small in his hand—a fob—and clicks the button. The silver light glowing through the far windows blinks out before blacklights kick on overhead, drenching the mansion in new colors. The gothic dark wallpaper all around us flares neon purple, patterned with my name repeating in black…

…just as the rose tattoo on his chest bursts into violent pink bloom.

"Tonight, I'm your reckoning."

CHAPTER 21

I react the way anyone would when they realize their dream has become a nightmare—I push him away and *sprint* down the hall like my life depends on it.

I need distance. I need time. I need a moment's peace to come to terms with what The Company has done to me.

But how can there be peace when Crimson suddenly calls out, "Run-Run-Run, little witch. There's no escaping us."

Heart pounding. Mind spiraling.

I round the promenade and stop short when I see Sky looming at the far end of the hall.

He…can't be Blake. Blake is dead.

Unless he isn't.

"Blake?"

He shakes his head. "Sky."

It should reassure me that they're actors—they're *all* actors and he's the only one willing to break character for this moment, to reassure me—but it does the opposite. If this was part of the play, he'd lie too, wouldn't he? And if he's not lying and they're not lying then…

I spin on the spot—right into Shadow's open arms. His fingers land on my shoulders and grip; white panic short-circuits every rational thought still left in my brain. I don't even think, I only react.

"No!" I scream as my knees fold beneath me and I crash-land on the floor, slipping right out of his grasp. Scrambling,

I crawl between his open legs and leap to my feet on the other side.

A laugh trails after me, dark and surprised, as I reach a staircase and stagger-stomp down them. I'm on the ground floor, moving, seconds later. I see a door to the back garden, but it's locked. And the second I pick up a pot to break the glass beside it, thunder and lightning conspire against me, roaring so loudly overhead, it scares me back. It's so loud, I almost can't hear the music anymore.

Music! The ballroom. The band!

I turn that direction, but…Crimson is *right there!*

His hands don't reach for my arms, or any such prosaic place. As if he's snatching a fly out of the air, one of his gargantuan hands snaps around my throat and tears me sideways before I can blink. With that one grip, he slams me into the nearest wall, knocking the wind out of me.

I half expect him to hold me at arm's length, but he does the opposite. He glues his body to mine in every way he can. There's no space at all, to breathe, to move, to even *attempt* to hit him.

His lips are against my cheek, his hands tighten on my throat and no amount of pushing can pry him off me. If anything, every push is met with a counter-push closer.

And a lick. A tiny flick of his tongue against my cheek.

A rub of himself against me. *He's turned on by this!*

But fuck, so am *I!*

"God, Ava," he purrs against my skin, summoning shivers. "You have *no idea* how long we searched for you."

"Stop it. Stop this!"

"Tell me you want me, baby," he begs, his voice low and deep.

"Get off!"

"Say it!" he demands, gently grazing his teeth across my cheekbone. "Tell me you *need* me."

I open my mouth to demand he let me go again, but no

words come out. He's right there, so close I can feel his panted warm breaths against my mouth. I can smell his natural scent faintly limned in peppermint and my body studders beneath me almost in warning.

And then he kisses me. It's hungry and desperate and so quick that when he pulls his lips away again, I mewl with need and try to chase them. But his grip on my throat won't let me.

"Admit you need me."

"No," escapes me in a whisper.

One of his hands leaves my throat and I feel a tangential tug at something between us. I don't realize what it is until I feel a soft slide and I hear his pants pool on the floor at his feet. Suddenly, his warm hardness is unignorable through the thin silk of my dress and cotton of his underwear. He wags himself against my hip, teasing.

"Admit you wanted us to show up tonight, Ava."

"No!" I whisper again.

"Admit you *hoped* it was really us."

I can't give in to that fucked-up part of myself. I can't, right? No, no. I can't. The last rational sane part of my brain knows it would be like diving headfirst into a delusion.

But my hands have minds of their own—*this is what you wanted*, they remind me... right before one wraps itself around his wrist while the other pretends to scratch at his hip for half a second before it slides into place on his bulge. Stroking, stroking. His warmth is so inviting, all I want to do is wrap my fingers around his—

"Where were you?" The words tear out of my throat like they belong to a scared little kid version of myself I locked away long ago. But I can't stop them. And once the words escape, sorrow taints the overwhelming lust clouding my thoughts. "Where were you!"

Crimson's eyes widen and his grip loosens, just the tiniest bit.

"They tore my clothes away and you were *right there!*" I shout at him. "You say you care about me, but where were you? Why didn't you leave that room and help me? They took everything—*everything*—from me and you let them!"

"Baby, baby, I'm sorry," he says, and it breaks my heart. All of it, the pet name, the earnest tone. "I am *so* sorry. I tried to leave. Blake grabbed me. Broke my nose. Then he started wailing on Sh—*Black Eyes*—and by the time I pulled them apart, you were already gone."

What? That can't be true. Can it?

"I came after you," he continues. "I ran into the woods shouting your name, but you never answered me. If you had..." He leans in, pressing his forehead to mine. "I would have *burned that fucking shack to the ground* with everyone in it if you'd asked me."

Fuck. I...I need...

I want...

I tear at his underwear, shoving it down, the same moment Crimson reaches for my dress and yanks it up. His hands leave my throat, unleashing a moan of injustice from me, but they're gone only long enough to hoist me up against the wall and wrap my legs around his hips. The second his beautiful thick cock slams inside me, his hands are around my throat again, tight and needy and so reassuring. So claiming.

So...indignant. Anger flashes across his beautiful eyes for a moment. Anger and relief together, mixing in some strange way as his brutal pace intensifies, spiking pleasure through the shattered whole of me. "This is your home, do you hear me?"

"W-What?" What is he talking about?

"This," he says, slamming his hips into me—again, *again, AGAIN!*—spiking pleasure through me so bad my legs shake around him. "Is *home*. Not the one you fucking abandoned back in Greenfield, or the one that abandoned you."

God, *fuck* him for reminding me of that! Fuck both of them for thinking an apology and some good dick make up for what I suffered.

With his hands around my throat, they can't catch my legs as I drop them from his waist and slam my hands upward against his arms, tearing them away from my throat before I shove him off. Crimson staggers back in surprise, his sherbert eyes melting with desire.

"Where did you learn *that* little move?" he asks.

I ignore him.

"Fuck your excuse, asshole," I pant. "Save your woulda-coulda-shouldas for somebody else. You wouldn't have done *jack shit* at that party."

I'm gone—running—before he can reply. I sprint for the front door, but Sky's already there, waiting, so I turn for the far hall beyond the ballroom, one I haven't visited before. High doorways frame grand salons to the right before I reach the dining room and the kitchen. I almost blow past it without a second thought, but this is a fancy house. The type of place where deliveries are probably made to the kitchen. I bet it has a door leading outside.

I skid into the doorway and race ahead, ignoring the sound of shattering glass as my hip takes out a waiter's tray of dozens of champagne flutes.

Grabbing the doorknob to what *must* be a side entrance, self-loathing tumbles out of my mouth, "*Stupid fat fuck.*"

"The fuck did you just say?"

I don't even turn at the sound of Crimson's voice. I twist the doorknob—even get it open an inch—before his massive hand *slams* into it right beside my head, shutting it again.

"What did I *fucking say* about insulting our girl, Ava?" he growls right against my ear. "This body? Your body? *Our* body? It's fucking perfect. Made for us."

His hands take hold of my arms before I can blink, and

pull them behind me, pinning them at the small of my back. He yanks me away from the door so fast I stagger—that's what he wants, I realize. He doesn't let me catch my balance before his other hand latches onto my hair and shoves my head forward, bending me over just enough before his hand pulls back and *smacks* the hill of my ass *once-twice-thrice!*

"Fuck!" I shout, at the surprise, at the bite of pain.

But more surprise greets me—he pauses for a microsecond before he yanks my dress up and he falls to his knee behind me. I feel lips against the tender skin. Soft, desperate kisses patter the heated sting.

"Is that better, baby?" he whispers. "Looks like Shadow got you good. Guess we'll have to aim for the other cheek, huh."

His lips land on the other cheek…right before his teeth bite down *hard* and he moans.

"Fuck you!" I roar, kicking back with my foot. It connects with his chest and his grip on my arms slips. I stumble forward out of his grasp. Then I'm moving again, around the kitchen island, for the far doorway.

"You will," he laughs. The sound penetrates the anger in me like nothing else. It's soft and delicious and…*patient?* He's enjoying this.

Fuck, so am I.

I leap through the doorway and spot Shadow turning the far corner and a delighted yelp leaves my lips before I can stop it. I turn on my heel, feeling the carpet *burn* my skin.

"Avaaaaa!" he yells.

I hate the sound of my name on his lips.

And I love it.

That low dulcet tone. That *need* I can hear to explain things he can't possibly explain.

But fuck if I'm going to tell him that. I reach the far doorway and pull myself through…into the ballroom where the musicians play on as if nothing is happening.

"Help!" I yell, stumbling forward. "I need a phone. I need—"

I feel hands on my arms from behind, then more hands on my legs, surrounding them, before I'm hoisted off my feet and carried back out. In the brief moment I can still see the musicians, though, I know there's no reason to return to them. They didn't bat an eye, they didn't stop playing. And I saw a chain link bracelet around the wrist of the guitarist.

They got the same rules I did, probably. Fuck.

I wiggle and wriggle and strain in their arms. I just need a give. Just a little give and I can—

"God, you're incredible," Crimson groans while trying to hold onto my legs. "Give us everything, baby."

"Put me down!"

Crimson laughs. "You heard her, Shadow."

I'm suddenly falling slowly, still unable to move in their torturous grip. I don't know how they do it, but they lower me to the hallway floor and Crimson has me pinned before I can get any leverage at all. He drops his ass onto mine, *sitting on me*, before grabbing my arms and twisting them behind my back.

"No! No!" I growl with everything I've got.

"That's the wrong word, sweetheart," Shadow says, stepping back to catch his breath as Crimson leans down, pressing himself to me.

His mouth is suddenly against my ear and he purrs, "Use the word you really mean and we'll give you everything you've ever dreamed of."

"Take the *fucking hint*!" I shout at them. "You think *any* of this makes up for that night?"

I expect some snarky reply…but they don't give me one. They're silent. Crimson's grip is unyielding, but he sits up and seems to freeze on top of me. Turning my head, I glance up to find them looking at each other, as if they're having some sort of silent fucking conversation.

"Oh, what's wrong, *baby*," I mock. "Finally figured out you failed me just as bad as the rest of them? Showing up *now* is showing up ten years too fucking late!"

The moment the words leave my mouth, a hand lands on my head, shoving it to the floor. Holding it there. I expect Crimson's voice against my ear again, but it's not him. It's Shadow, and he sounds...devastated?

"Don't say that," he growls through gritted teeth. "There's no *too late* for us, do you hear me? Not after everything we've done to find you. After we—"

"Shadow!" Crimson barks, but Shadow's voice cuts him off halfway through the word, "No, hold her still. It's listening time now."

The pressure on my head lightens and there's suddenly a hand under my head, cushioning it. Shadow's lips crash against my temple, pattering unforgiving kiss after kiss as he takes a moment to brush the sweat-soaked hairs plastered to my face. It's...tender...and strange...and confusing.

"W-What are you doing?" I whisper.

His lips are there again before I can even recoil. "Ava, we can't do anything about being late to help you. But we were there. *We were there, sweetheart!* We saw you destroy that fucking prick's face with that stone. We saw you crush that asshole's balls. *So. Fucking. Perfect.* Except that you ran too fast. You were gone too quick! If you'd just turned when we called for you, you would've seen us there taking care of the rest of it for you."

It's my turn to freeze. Crimson loosens his hold on me, I think because he can feel the struggle leaving my body. I raise my head so I can study Shadow's eyes through the mask while he stares me down, *begging* me to believe him without him explicitly saying what I think he's saying.

But I have to know for sure. "How did you take care of the rest of it?"

"Let's just say Blake didn't walk himself off that

cliff…and a bloody stone sinks as fast as a clean one."

Some hot angry biting thing in my chest—something that's been there so long it feels lodged in my internal wall—gives way. It releases its grip and dislodges, leaving a gaping raw wound behind. Tears rush in to fill the abscess.

"You killed Blake?"

A warm smile curves across Shadow's stubbled face. Then Crimson is there as if he can't stand to be excluded. His hands release my arms and band around my chest, pulling me up a little so he can kiss my hair-head-shoulder.

"*Of course* we did," he swears so softly. "You think anyone who does that to our girl gets to live?"

"If you'd *just waited* for us, we would've told you everything," Shadow says. "But you were already gone by the time we got to your house. You disappeared like a fucking pro, sweetheart."

I smile at that. I don't know why, the compliment hits just right. The smile he gives me in return is so open and relieved and *happy* to see my happiness—it's beautiful.

"You searched for me?"

"*Fuck* did we search for you," Shadow growls, eyes blowing wide with a frustration so scratchy I can almost feel it against my skin. "*Six cities*, Ava. And everywhere our work took us."

Crimson chuckles in my ear, raising every goosebump on my body. His eyes dart playfully to Shadow. "You had this hopeful fuck chasing down every brunette baddie with thicc thighs and a decadent double-decker ass he saw. Had to watch him get his hopes wrecked a thousand times looking for you."

"After you disappeared, we made Emily's life a nightmare until her folks pulled her out of school."

"You did?"

Shadow nods again and says, "We torched her car and set her prom dress on fire. Got her parents fired from their jobs eventually too."

"Among other things," Crimson teases, drawing my attention to him. "Let's just say a letter of un-recommendation always seems to find its way into her boss's inbox a few months after she starts working at a new place."

"And if that doesn't work, we stir the pot in other ways."

"You've kept track of her all these years?" I ask.

"Hardly an effort," Shadow says. "She lays her entire life out on social media."

"Unlike you," Crimson croons. "Little witch? More like little ghost."

I feel the tight chains I'd locked around my heart long ago begin to loosen.

They seem to sense it. All the desperation on Shadow's face, and the snark on Crimson's, fades to...*intensity*. Quiet intensity only enhanced by those beautiful faceted masks on their faces.

And in that silence...*need*. Hunger. Desire worth burning alive for.

I can't stop looking at Shadow's lips, at Crimson's. Back and forth, I can't stop until I'm panting.

"What? No snarky reply?" Shadow asks.

"Fuck you," I say, but with a different sort of bite.

"We know that's what you want," Crimson growls against my ear, so low and deep, rubbing his rigid cock slowly—decadently—against my ass. "Say it."

"Damn it, I..."

"Say it, Ava," Shadow commands.

"I want you to fuck me!"

"You fucking need us."

"Yes! Yes, I fucking need you to fuck me!"

The sound Crimson makes; i-it's not what I expect. I expect triumph. I expect pride.

What I get is, "Ah, fuck!"

It escapes him in desperation. Impatient *pain*. As if he

can't stand the millimeters of distance between our bodies. As if I was the one who had him pinned and immobile on the floor.

But he's not anymore.

He's not. And neither is his insane quivering cock.

His hand gropes for the hem of my dress, scratching my skin as he tears it up over my ass.

There's a breeze.

And a purr of pure indulgence before—

"Holy fuck!"

His cock conquers my ass like a battering ram. It plunges inside so fast, I shriek! The rose plug helped. It helped, but it wasn't as meaty as he is. It wasn't as needy. As desperate. As relentless.

His arms swoop around my chest, pinning my arms to my side. Then he rises into squat, bringing my upper body with him, all while he plunges into me again and again.

It's war. My body's at war with him. With what he's doing to me. Pleasure and pain. Awareness and mindlessness. The whimper of me clashing against the aching roar of him.

I'm helpless, hanging in the air as he pounds into me from behind. The only parts of me touching the floor are my knees-calves-feet. The rest of me is dangling. Held. Constricted within his arms, at the mercy of his insatiable cock's need to be inside me…and inside me again.

"Yes-Yes-Yes," becomes his whispered chant against my ear. "Take it-Take it-Take it. Just take it."

And then fingers land on my clit, strumming-strumming-strumming, and the pleasure eeks out the pain, transforming it into a slow burning fuse slithering across the expanse of me, promising ecstasy, promising destruction, promising an explosion that destroys me. It's all I can feel. All I can f-f-feel.

I-I can't think.

I can barely see!

His invasion is neverending. N-N-Never…end-d-d-ing. Unceasing. A religious crusade against everything I thought I knew about…about…

"Oh. My. Goddddddd!"

"That's it, baby," Crimson moans. "So fucking perfect."

"Almost."

Fingers brush over my cheeks. My eyes snap open to find Shadow there, studying my face so strangely while Crimson uses me. I can barely keep my eyes open, but as my eyelids alternate their slow-blinks, I realize he's delicately sweeping the hairs out of my face again.

So gentle.

He kisses me so gently in the onslaught…

Before two of his fingers are there at my mouth and plunge inside across the wet expanse of my tongue.

Fuck, he pushes. He pushes them down to the back of my throat, and when I gag, he groans with excitement. Again and again, his fingers plumb the depths of my mouth…and Crimson watches, his pace quickening with anticipation.

But it's hard to catch my breath. Between the thrusts that drive the breath out of me and the wiggling fingers that have me gasping for air and the fact that I can't move my head, can't move my *body*.

Merciless. It's *merciless*!

Until suddenly—

Shadow takes his fingers away and I suck in oxygen like I may never get it again.

He rises to stand, still fisting my hair…

And his free hand lowers to his pants. A quick zip and tug and the curtain falls on his civility, unveiling his glorious cock. It drops in front of my face, almost wagging for me to pay attention—as if I could look away!

"Open." The word is so low and graveled, for a moment I think his cock is speaking to me.

"W-What?"

His fist in my hair tightens and yanks. Just a little. Just enough to wake me out of the fucking *cock-coma* Crimson's trapped me in.

"You're gonna take this cock, Ava. You're gonna swallow me down and you're gonna look at me while you do it. Keep your beautiful eyes on me, sweetheart."

Again, the words are...I can't think with this dick in my ass!

"*Wha—*"

My traitorous lips never finish the word. Because his cock is there—here! Parting my lips wide. Plunging deep. Pressing at my soft palate, then deeper. Deeper until my jaw begins to ache and my throat begins to tighten.

"Fucking hell."

He pulls back barely half an inch before he pushes a little deeper and a sound escapes him that makes my pussy quiver. I take as much of him as I can, trying to keep my eyes on his beautiful dark-ashen gaze in the midst of everything else. I can barely do it. Barely do it because Crimson *hasn't fucking paused once* and my eyes are glossing over with tears even though I'm the happiest I think I've ever been.

Then Crimson bites my earlobe and Shadow groans again and fuck if I'm not so fucking close to coming, I don't know what to do with myself.

Almost. It's right there.

Release is *right there*!

But then Shadow pulls all the way out of my mouth and all I can do is mewl with protest. With *anger*.

"Fucking hell, where are you going?" I bark.

Shadow smirks. His hold on my hair shifts, forcing me to look down at his dick, where he has his free hand wrapped around it only halfway up the shaft.

"Is that all you can take, sweetheart?" he teases.

Fuck, the taunt makes me shiver.

"I took it deeper than that," I pant.

"Oh, you will," Shadow says.

"Guess we'll have to train her," Crimson adds, landing a soft kiss on my head. "We'll start tomorrow."

"Tomorrow? There *is* no—"

But I never get to finish. I can't. Crimson continues his ruthless assault on my ass as Shadow shoves himself down my throat again. I try to pull back, try to get a breath, but there just isn't any as I stare up into the dark mesmerizing ashen eyes of my Shadow and let him fuck my face until his eyes and mouth blow wide with reverence and he begins to pray, "My *fucking* God!"

Crimson echoes it with his murmured, purred, "Yes-yes-*yes*, baby."

I think this might be the holy fuck they promised me.

The pleasure, their hold on me, the inability to catch my fucking breath—it all unravels me. Pulls the last loose thread on this whole charade and everyone involved. Real, not real, who could bother qualifying?

*This—them plundering my body, whispering and groaning and roaring and demanding—*is absolute.

Merciless.

Except for the way Crimson strokes my clit. Except for the way Shadow pulls back when he thinks I'm close to passing out. Except for the way they both make time to kiss my temple, to stroke my cheek so fucking softly.

They're watching me unravel. They're catching the threads as they come loose. They're more aware of me than I am aware of anything.

Whispering: "This is what you were made for, little witch."

Growling: "Tell us you love us with my cock down your throat…louder!…scream it around my cock!"

My garbled, muffled scream of a response only spurs them on.

And I'm grateful for it. *I'm grateful for the onslaught!* I don't want it to stop. I can't imagine it stopping—

But Crimson pauses his plundering suddenly and I-I don't know what to do as he lowers my body to the floor and leaves my person altogether. Shadow, too, finally leaves my throat.

It's a break I desperately need and hate with every inch of my body.

I can't help but mewl weakly in protest…because that's all I have left in me. My eyes are still fluttering against the aftershocks of pleasure. My body's trembling. I couldn't walk now if I tried.

"Patience," Shadow coos, so pleased with himself. "We're not done yet."

Shadow lands behind me on the floor and rolls me onto my side facing away, hugging me so gently as he catches his breath and nibbles the skin of my neck.

"Look," he hums breathlessly. "Look at how Crimson cares for you."

I can barely focus, until Shadow cradles my head and slightly turns me to where my Crimson is standing. But when my eyes finally grasp him, it's still another few seconds to understand that he's…

He's…cleaning his dick. Carefully. Thoughtfully. With actual soap and water from a bowl on the end table. Where did that even come from?

"We take good care of our woman," Shadow promises against my skin, then against my lips with the strangest, gentlest kiss.

By the time my eyes catch on Crimson again, his eyes are red with lust and his cock looks…too clean. He pops open a drawer on a nearby end table and pulls out another bottle of lube, which he brings with him as he strolls toward us, raking his heavy-lidded gaze across my body. He flicks the top of the bottle open, pouring a bit into his palm before tossing the bottle to Shadow, and I…

I realize this was some sort of deliciously patient intermission for them. For me.

And I should already be on my feet running again.

I should. I should.

If only my feet would cooperate…

But the second I put any pressure on my toes, they slip out from under me.

And Crimson chuckles. "No need to put on a show for us, little witch. You're exactly where we want you."

He lowers himself down in front of me, just as Shadow nuzzles closer from behind. Shadow's lube-slick fingers bring his glorious cock to my ass as Crimson's meaty cock arrives at my cunt, and the anticipation of what's about to happen has me shivering before either presses inside.

And when they do? *Fuck*, I feel them everywhere. The fullness of them both inside me takes my breath away again, obliterates my thoughts, nukes any control I have over my body. Shadow has his relentless fucking way with me as Crimson slams inside my soaking wet pussy, spearing himself deep, giving my pussy exactly what she needs to lose her fucking mind.

And when I finally come—when the fuse finally detonates that twisted decade-deep pit of dynamite inside me—they fill me with themselves as if they were always just waiting for me to get there.

It's a climax I've waited ten years for…and the explosion steals me from the waking world in a fiery expansion of mindless, ecstatic pleasure. So bright and big and relentless I can only ride it out and hope to make it through.

And when darkness finally seizes me, I know only one thing is true in this world—I'm gonna have to win *a lot* of big cases moving forward.

The Company has me now. I don't know how long it'll be before I call them again; I only know that I *will* call. And whatever my fantasy, it'll be worth every penny.

CHAPTER 22

THIRTY-SIX HOURS LATER

"Ms. St. Jude."

"Mmff?"

"Ms. St. Jude, can you hear me? Open your eyes, sweetheart."

Sweetheart? Nobody calls me sweetheart except Shadow...but this isn't Shadow. A woman's here with me.

Prying my dry, tired eyes open should qualify me for sainthood. When they finally give, my first thought is that I must be in a hospital. A very posh hospital.

The light is soft, through semi-thick taupe curtains. The walls are the same color, as is everything in the room, including the coat on the older woman checking the IV stand by my bed. She looks like a chic grandmother with a warm, non-judgmental smile to match. Musak is playing, a harp and piano I think; it's so soft I wonder if it's some bit of dream I dragged with me back into the waking world.

"Good afternoon, Ms. St. Jude."

Afternoon? My dark escorts really must've taken a lot out of me.

Nope, they definitely did; I feel soreness and strain tugging at my limbs as I begin to bend and stretch against the soft mattress. As if I ran an ultra-marathon. My ass, too, is...tender, although I think they might have given me something for that because there's no pain.

My body feels deliciously exhausted...

Entirely satisfied…

And horny again, I can't believe it.

Or maybe I can. Memories jostle for attention at the front of my mind. Hands and lips and masks and sherbert eyes and glorious cocks that couldn't get enough of me.

Then the thought of the revenge I got on Emily comes crashing in like some sort of twisted cherry on top!

Fuck!

"Don't rush yourself, just take your time adjusting, all right?" she says, adding, "I'm taking out your IV now. Just a slight pinch."

I barely feel it in the midst of…everything else.

"Where am I?"

"In a spa just a few minutes from your home. We outfitted this recovery room for you, so take as long as you need today to decompress. Have a massage. Get a facial. When you're ready to leave, one of our drivers will take you home, all right? Just don't forget your goodie bag when you go."

She motions to a luxe taupe gift bag sitting on a table nearby. Beautiful, save for the very distinct logo emblazoned on the side in blood red—broken chain links wrapped around the words *concede voluptati—surrender to pleasure*. The Company's logo.

"Inside, you'll find a salve for…more sensitive parts of your body and your now-deactivated chain bracelet to have as a keepsake. You'll also find information about our upcoming events so you can let us know which you'll be available to participate in."

"So soon?"

Her smile is enigmatic. "We don't take our lifelong memberships lightly. Just remember to pick up the phone when we call."

I glance at her then, unsure whether that's a warning or a promise.

She smiles as if she knows it's both. "The Company's

always there, when you're ready to call them again, too."

I nod; it's all I can do. I know what I joined, what they expect of me moving forward. And after what they did for me? I *want* to help make someone else's fantasy come true.

But she studies me for a moment, and I know a question is coming before she asks. "Was it everything you hoped it would be?"

A tightness strains the back of my throat as I nod and whisper, "Better."

Her shrug is a blasé thing, but I can see right through it to the pride underneath. Her eyes sparkle with it.

"A lot of what we do is little more than theater, Ms. St. Jude. Cosplay. Roleplay. Curiosity and kink and fun. A taste of the abnormal for those with otherwise ordinary lives. But every so often we get a client who needs...more. For those, fantasy is the sweet coating on the medicine they're really asking for. Once that fantasy melts away, what they're left with is the truth they've been running from for far too long."

I smile at that. "Are you saying the chase I asked for was something else?"

"I'm saying that chases end one of two ways—either you're caught...or you keep running forever. In your case, you let them catch you. Quite quickly, in fact. Maybe you should ask yourself why."

Why.

I don't think that's a question I can answer in a day.

Certainly not while I'm recovering from the sinful things my dark gentlemen did to me. Sure, I get a facial. Sure, the massage is *divine* and works out (most of) the kinks my escorts left behind. But I spend half my time pleasuring myself to thoughts of...all of it...mulling over that question she left me with. Playing with it. Reliving the best moments of that night while they're still fresh.

Fuck, I know exactly what the partner at my firm was talking about...about the fantasy haunting her long after it ended. And I'm glad it's so vivid for me still, as I gingerly lower myself into the backseat of the town car that's waiting for me outside the spa.

I'm glad I can remember.

I'm going to write everything down when I get home, so I can revisit my fantasy for many years to come.

Honestly, I don't think I could forget if I tried.

I don't want to.

Because beneath all the bliss and relief and fucking *healing* I feel after that night, there's also a sour twinge of sadness to contend with. And it doesn't have anything to do with the fact that I passed out before I could have Sky— although, I feel like I should get a partial refund for that!

The sadness is attached to her question, I think, and its answer.

My Crimson. My Shadow.

The Company did an *immaculate* job preparing them.

Fuck, they knew so much.

They made me believe they were real! By the end, I really thought they were my Red-Eyes and Black-Eyes, that they'd been searching for me all along. I'd never imagined that detail, never entertained that possibility. My fantasy had been wholly mine before they said that!

But once that entered the play, *fuck* if I didn't crave it. Every time they called me baby and sweetheart. Every time they swore they'd gone half mad looking for me. I wanted that to be true. It took the fantasy beyond the physical and *claimed my brain* until surrendering to this *perfect version* of that night from long ago was all I could do!

The Company's credo—*surrender to pleasure*—was exactly right. When I finally did? *My God!*

Next time, I'll surrender faster.

Knowing me, I'll probably surrender *too* fast and mess up my fantasy a different way.

But the sadness is there for the exact same reason I'm

happy. They were incredible...and fleeting. They're gone and I'll never see them again. Or maybe I will, walking down some street somewhere. I'll see the angle of their jaw on a man passing by, or make eyes at someone from across a smoky bar and wonder if he's one of the actors they hired for me.

I *know* I'll be ogling every man with neck tattoos, searching for storm cloud tats for the rest of my life!

Fuck, the loss of them is...nothing like I expected. I actually miss them. I knew I couldn't keep them before this started, and yet parts of me feel their absence like a bruise that's slow to heal. My heart. My empty arms. My pussy...*fuck* does she miss them.

The woman was right; I let Crimson and Shadow catch me. I *wanted* them to catch me—of course I did; the O.G. fantasy demanded it.

But them needing me? It left a buzz under my skin. A new craving even stronger than the first.

I *still* want them to need me.

Which is...silly.

And amazing—no wonder The Company has repeat customers!

A few minutes later when the driver pulls up in front of my condo, I thank him as quickly as I can, already aiming for my large warm bed and the vibrator I keep in my bedside drawer. Thank fuck The Company already arranged for me to have several days off with my firm; I think it'll take that long for my pussy to stop screaming for men she can never have again!

But...

As I walk up my ordinary condo stairs in my ordinary quiet neighborhood, something tears me from my indecent dreaming.

My front door is standing wide open.

And leaning to either side of the open doorway...are two

masks—one that looks like smokey quartz and one that looks like a faceted ruby.

My heart seizes inside me. I glance back at the car, at the driver; he's watching me. He nods as if all of this is entirely normal before he drives away, leaving me to...the reality of those masks.

That open doorway.

I don't know what to do. Do I leave? Do I call Lucy? Or The Company? Or the cops?

I'm frozen on the front path, trying to decide what this could possibly mean. The night is over. The fantasy is finished.

Isn't it?

Buzz...Buzz...Buzz...

The noise is quiet—nothing more than vibration against fabric—but I hear it all the same. There on the welcome mat—a cell phone. *My* cell phone.

I reach it just as the buzz dies. A call from an unmarked number.

And then...a text.

Welcome home, baby.

Then another.

Hope you don't mind, but we got ourselves settled while you were away.

A strange noise of confusion leaves my mouth.

Who is this? I text.

Guess. I'll give you a reward if you're right. I am the echo of your body, dark and faithful.

My heart squeezes inside me, as I reply, *Shadow?*

:) You're just full of surprises.

The shock I feel is soured with fear and sweetened with joy—a joy I have *no* business feeling!

I ask the only question that comes to mind, *Are you in my home right now?*

His answer chills and boils my blood. *Our home.*

I…turn. My foot pivots to run—

When a string of texts comes in, back and forth, back and forth from them.

Uh-uh-uh. Run and we'll chase you, Ava St. Jude.

You think we searched for ten years for a single night with you?

Once wasn't enough.

Forever isn't enough.

Come home, baby.

We've been waiting for you for so long.

Choose us.

Come find us.

Run and we'll chase you.

Happy to.

Run and we'll chase you.

If that's what you want.

But we know what you really need…is to be caught.

Run or surrender, Ava. Either way this ends the same.

With our cocks inside you.

With our arms around you.

Together like we've always wanted. Forever.

Fuck, don't you want that too?

Don't you want us, baby?

Run or surrender, sweetheart. It's up to you.

CHAPTER 23

I know I should run. Fuck, I *know* I should.

This doesn't end with Happily Ever After. I knew that before I joined The Company. I was *prepared* for that! I said goodbye to Crimson, Shadow, and Sky before I even met them.

But now?

They're blowing up my phone with sweet, dark promises that stick to my skin like blood, like darkness. Promises of everything they can offer me if I step into my own condo and chase *them* this time.

There are just two problems with that—that's not how this works, and I'm a practical creature.

My heart and pussy can whine at me all night long; my brain knows better.

No one should be in my home without my permission.

I turn to run, because that's what I *should* do.

I turn to run—

"Wrong choice, little witch."

A hand is around my throat. Lips land against mine with a softness *completely at odds* with the claiming grip on my neck. And I'm moving backward, through my own front door before I can blink.

Before I can scream!

It closes and locks while I'm still trying to claw myself free of the hand. His hand. But it barely phases him. Not even when I draw blood.

"Ow, Ava!" the man deadpans, almost as if to a child.

"Let me go!"

"You would be so disappointed in me if I did, baby."

He's maskless. He's *beautiful*. Crimson, I realize. The almond eyes that look like melting sherbert are there, just out of reach for clawing. They're smiling at me, watching me squirm helplessly in his grip. And the rest of his face. Same bitable angular jaw, same dark tousled hair. But the cheekbones. They're as high as I thought they must be under his mask. And his brow is pronounced.

Lovely.

His smile eeks up one side of his face, almost tenderly, as he realizes what I'm thinking. Right before he startles me with, "God, you're so beautiful."

"Always was," Shadow says, pulling my focus.

He's…shirtless in my home, leaning against the wall close to the kitchen so casually, as if he's lived here for years. That rose tattoo on his chest is on full display, and real, I think. His mask is gone too…and my knees almost give underneath me.

The dirty blond hair is combed and still wet from a shower, falling just to his cheeks, which are round and *beautiful* under his black-arson eyes.

But that's not the reason my knees almost give out. *I recognize him.* I recognize the teenager I once knew…from Mr. Lawson's class. He's obviously older, and the acne that once crowded his cheeks has become light scarring, but age has revealed how handsome I always thought he was. There are also two little symmetrical beauty marks—one under each eye—that I've never seen on anyone else. Marks I used to tease him about when we were in class.

"…Shane? Shane Blackwell?"

"Miss me, Ava?" he asks.

"Just your birthmarks."

It's what I used to say to him on Mondays when he'd ask me if I missed him over the weekend. At least, it was something I had started saying to him near the end, right before I had to flee. We were...getting friendlier. Closer. Fuck, he was the only person at that school who was remotely nice to me. Which of course meant I had a crush on him! As much of one as I would allow myself to have; I never thought that he liked me. Why would he, with my greasy hair and shitty life?

Shane rewards me with a smile I recognize too, in hindsight. But...something's different about him, and I can't help asking, "What happened to your voice?"

It's deeper, raspier than it once was.

"Smoking." He grimaces playfully at me, and turns a little, revealing a nicotine patch on the back of his arm. "I'm quitting for you. I swear."

"I'll keep him honest," Crimson teases, drawing my attention back to him, which isn't easy considering he's still got his massive fingers wrapped firmly around my throat.

But this time, he's holding me at a distance for a different reason. Because I'm looking at him. I'm really *looking* at him. I reach out and graze my fingertips softly along the angular jaw, up to his beautiful brow. He gulps against my scrutiny, as if he's nervous about what I'll think when I figure out who he is...

Or maybe he's assuming I won't be able to.

It's his lips and brow that give him away, though, which is funny considering when I knew him in school, his hair was long, hiding his forehead completely. I only knew he *had* a brow ridge because Blake tripped him one day in the hallway and I offered him a hand up off the floor.

Otherwise, I only ever saw him in the cafeteria, avoiding people's gaze, working on a laptop covered in stickers. And sometimes when I didn't have enough money for lunch, I'd find a cup of peaches or an apple or a sweet cake sitting on the table I usually sat at alone. I only ever caught him leaving gifts for me once, but once I knew it was him, I...couldn't help but watch him from time to time wondering why.

"Chris."

The moment the name leaves my mouth, his grip on my throat loosens in surprise. "Chris Velmorne."

"You remember me?" he asks.

"Of course I do."

And I suddenly understand how they kept themselves a secret throughout my fantasy, and at that party ten years ago. Shane wasn't shy about talking to me in class but as Black-Eyes, he never said a word to me. And Chris? Well...he never spoke to me in school. Not once. Not about the food he sometimes gave me. Not even when I helped him up off the floor. He just nodded and rushed past me. I thought I'd embarrassed him by helping him. But as Red-Eyes, he did enough talking for the pair of them.

"Shane mentioned once that you prefer to be called Christy."

His eyes close as the name leaves my lips; relief washes over his face. His hand slides to the side of my neck before pulling me into his chest, enveloping me in an embrace so tight it's like he's trying to touch our souls together.

I can't help but nestle into it; I fit in his arms as if I was made for them, as if he was made for me.

"Is that what you want me to call you?" I whisper gently.

"Call me whatever you want. Just, whatever you call me, say it loud and *often*, okay?"

Then Shane is there, rubbing my back, a smile on his face so bright it's like seeing the sun for the first time. "See? I told you she'd remember. He may look like a killer—he may *be* a killer—but he's just a big softy really."

"Shut up," Christy chuffs with amusement.

But...the casual admission of *that* makes me realize *everything* they told me that night might be true.

"Did you really kill Blake?"

"Of course we did," Christy swears so sincerely. "Ten seconds. If you'd stayed another ten seconds, Ava, this would've all been different."

I believe him. It's madness. It's insanity…but I believe him.

Stepping back, I reach for Shane, to pull him in so they can both surround me, smother me.

"You're here now," I whisper, luxuriating in their closeness.

"We're here forever," Shane counters.

I feel the smile on my face before the happiness registers in my heart, my mind, my soul. It's madness. It's insanity. I know it is, but…

"What does that look like?" I ask.

"To start?" Christy reaches for the button on my pants and pops it with relish.

"We're going to fuck the last bit of resistance out of you," Shane says, yanking my shirt away.

"Right before you smother me with your gorgeous fucking thighs and sit on my face until you come."

"And then, we're making you waffles. If that's all right with you, sweetheart."

Fuck, it's *more* than all right. Especially as my pants pool on the floor a second before Shane's hands are on my waist, lifting me out of them. Then a fist is in my hair, twisting, shoving me toward my couch.

Christy forces me onto the armrest, belly down…at the perfect height to—

"Ah! Careful!"

"Is that tender?" Christy asks, running his fingers over my back entrance, which is still sore from how desperately they fucked me on that hallway floor. When I nod, he whispers, "Baby, I'm sorry. You should have said something."

"She couldn't," Shane smirks. "Her mouth was a little

preoccupied."

Christy's hands clutch my hips, almost reeling at the thought. "Fuck and the way her bubbly ass bounced for us?"

Shane licks his fingers and runs them over my asshole soothingly. "She's not used to us yet. We'll have to take better care of her."

"They gave me a salve," I say, motioning to the little bag lying on its side in the foyer.

"Then after we're done, I'll apply it for you," he says. "Is your pussy still tender?"

No. My pussy—fuck, she's *roaring* for him. Them. I shake my head, watching over my shoulder as Christy undoes his pants, and Shane whips off his belt. Then their cocks are there, pearls of pre-cum catching in the sunlight, and Christy's fingers plunge deep inside me.

"She's soaking wet for us," Christy growls under his breath. "I'm on top."

"Fuck yeah, go for it."

On top, as compared to what? The words crowd my mouth, ready to fire, but they never make it out. They never make it because Christy plunges his thick fucking cock into my pussy without a warning, without a clue, without a single moment's hesitation. It fills me.

I moan again as my pussy muscles almost suckle at his cock, pulsing around it.

He pushes himself deep, then even *deeper*, before he suddenly leans over me, pressing himself to my back. His leg rears up on the couch beside mine, and his arms wrap under my arms and take hold of my shoulders, as if bracing for something. His head lands against mine, pressing it to the armrest and then his lips are there pattering soft *kiss-kiss-kisses* against my head.

"God, you feel so good—*three days without you was too long*." he hums right before he says, "Ready..." but not to me.

"I'm going slow," Shane replies, but...I...

"Slow?" I beg.

More soft pecking kisses rain down on my head...as I feel Shane's glorious fucking cock press against my clit...before pushing up into my pussy beside Christy's.

"Wait-Wait-WAIT!"

I'm already full.

I'm already full!

But there *is* no waiting. I don't think they can hear me over the double-groan of lust that escapes them the second Shane seats himself inside me.

Oh God, it's madness. Oh God, it's insane.

And then they begin to move. They *both* begin to pound my pussy together as if they can't resist and can't slow down and can't imagine stopping. The thunderous impact. The monsoon wetness. It's a perfect fucking storm in my pussy. My mind fractures. I scream gibberish! I scream with blissful madness, insane overstimulation.

F-F-Fuck, I feel so...so...fucking...*satisfied*.

My brain is gone, replaced by *feeling*. There's nothing else. The feeling of their cocks p-p-pumping inside me. The feeling of impossibly soft, gentle fucking kisses on my head. And fingernails skimming across the wide expanse of my ass. And then teeth on my shoulder as Christy bites down, growling.

"You love this?" Shane asks, and I barely hear him.

Until he slaps my ass, demanding an answer, and I cry out, "Yes, YES! Don't ever fucking stop."

I'm spiraling, completely out of it when the next question catches me off guard.

"You love us?"

"What?" I barely manage.

"Say it like you said it with my cock down your throat. Like you mean it."

"But—"

"Say it again so we can hear it," Christy echoes. "Loud and clear, little witch. Loud and fucking clear before you can't anymore."

Fuck, it's an impossible question.

"It's too soon," I whimper.

"What? Speak up, baby."

"It's too soon," I beg.

SLAP! SLAPSLAP! Against my ass, like fucking strikes of lightning.

"Say it," Shane commands, but I won't. Not this time. Not in *my* fucking house.

"No!" I yell. "You have to fucking earn it."

And it's...

It's as if I issued them some sort of challenge. Shane's fingers glide into place along my clit, strumming, and Christy's hand grips my throat again and he moans right into my ear as their pace intensifies. *Intensifies.*

The kisses.

The fucking.

The surrender to a pleasure I've never known.

Whoever Ava St. Jude was before The Company got ahold of her is long gone, replaced by a being of pure pleasure and madness, plundered by strangers promising impossibly lovely things.

"Oh, we will," they swear breathlessly against my skin. "You bet we fucking will."

THE END

The *Dark Encounters series consists of standalone novellas exploring the fantasies clients hire The Company to fulfill.*

Please find a sneak preview of the next book below.

His Perfect Plaything

CHAPTER 1

"Betony, there are only two types of people in this world—nosey fuckers like us…and those with something to hide."

It's too early for this.

I don't exactly know what *this* is yet, but my boss, Daniel, knows better than to summon me to the office at such an ungodly hour without good cause.

I can already tell he has one when he smiles and adds, "That's why we'll always have a job."

"It's seven in the morning, Daniel," I say anyway, although I can't keep the teasing tone out of my voice. We both know I would—and have—gone without sleep for days to score a good story. The articles for which I've won National Headliner and Livingston awards leer at me from places of honor on Daniel's office walls …even though they're bound to get replaced the second someone in the office wins a Pulitzer.

Yes, that someone will be me, if I have anything to say about it.

But right now, I'm covering a deep wide yawn with the back of my hand. I didn't even have time to grab coffee before I came in.

"Something's come up and I need my best reporter on it," Daniel says with a sly twinkle in his eye. "Something to do with a certain disgustingly handsome, devious, shadowy puppeteer we all love to hate."

That wakes me right up.

"Sam Eversleigh?"

"The String-Puller himself. Mr. God."

Most people in the western world wouldn't know his name. They wouldn't know his face. And yet he's impacted every single one of their lives. He's... "The man who runs the world."

"That's the one," Daniel hums. His tone gives me pause too; Daniel only gets quiet when he's hunting and has caught a scent. Right now, he's quiet as a mouse.

"What's the story?"

"I have no idea. I only know that he's recently made a very peculiar request through some sort of dark web community, one that had my spidey-senses tingling the moment I read it."

"What did it say?"

"*'I'm in need of a new marionette.'* Then there were a set of dates."

"What dates?"

"An entire month, starting next Tuesday."

My mind scrolls through random tidbits of gossip I've heard circulating around D.C. in recent weeks until it lands on the relevant info. "Eversleigh cleared his entire month for R&R..."

"Which is, of course, a euphemism for being busier than ever. My contact at the Pentagon says there's something going down in the Middle East and it's pulling focus from half a dozen other operations. Eversleigh is participating. *Pfft*, he's probably running the entire thing."

"Do you think 'marionette' is code for some cover op then?"

"Don't know. That's why I called you."

I snort in disbelief. In all the years I've known Daniel, he's *never* voluntarily given away a big scoop he could have taken for himself.

"Why?" I ask.

"Because next Tuesday, some sort of audition is happening. I managed to find the recruitment firm running it but...I'm ineligible to apply."

I realize why half a second later. "It's only open to women."

"Attractive, young women with squeaky clean backgrounds."

I frown at that. "I don't have a squeaky clean anything."

"The persona we crafted for you does."

His hand lands on a red file on his desk and shoves it toward me lightly, beckoning me to take a look. When I do, I'm greeted by an altered photo of myself—one in which my face appears on the body of an entirely different woman...or a body generated by AI. I'm...she's...wearing a soft pink dress patterned with cherries with a matching headband holding back her dark hair. It's giving volunteer candy striper, and though there's nothing wrong with that, this is a very specific look for a very specific kind of man. I feel my hackles rise at the suggestion that this is who he expects me to be.

"Betty Brie," I say, reading my persona's name. "She's a homebody who likes to bake, read, and..." *Ugh*, the end of the sentence makes me want to violently roll my eyes. "...pleasure herself several times a day."

Daniel shrugs at me. "Sounds like the only difference between the two of you is your name."

That's...not entirely untrue. It's not fair either, but...Daniel's known me a long time. Long enough to know I've been a bit of a sexually repressed recluse lately.

"Look, you're the only person in the entire office who refuses to have a social media presence, which works in our favor to conceal your real identity. You're also attractive, capable, and not squeamish when it comes to doing uncomfortable things to ferret out the truth. That's what I'm looking for..."

I eye him at that.

"In the reporter I send," he adds quickly. "The bullshit about baking and whatever was added based on what we know about his past girlfriends."

"And the sexual stuff?" I ask, raising an eyebrow.

"'Marionette' could mean anything, but a powerful man like that using some illicit service to find a certain type of woman...? We hedged our bets."

"You don't expect me to sleep with him, do you?"

Daniel only shrugs again. "We'll be in constant contact with you, and we'd pull you out the second you couldn't hack it anymore, but otherwise... It's your circus. If the monkeys get too rowdy, you can burn the whole tent down, call it quits, and come back. But...if you discover the lion tamer's feeding bodies to the lion, well, how far you go is up to you."

I lean back in my chair, mulling over the proposition. I wouldn't even consider it under normal circumstances— nevermind the ethical implications of seducing someone for a story; there are plenty of dark scenarios a private ad from one of the world's most dangerous and powerful men could trap me in. And if he ever found out who I really was...?

But it's Sam Eversleigh.

No one really knows him. Not even us. If I qualify as a lurker on social media, by contrast he doesn't exist at all. Except he does. Since I started working for the paper five years ago, his name has been attached to some of the biggest political moves of the century.

I might learn nothing.

Or everything.

And working on *one* story—as opposed to trying to satisfy the bottomless maw of digital media consumption like I've been doing nonstop for the last five years—sounds like a break I've desperately needed for quite some time.

"Suppose a month's vacation could be nice," I say, almost aside to myself.

"That's the spirit," Daniel says. "I'll even send you home now to…start your own research."

"Will I get a wardrobe budget? A list of things I'll need for this?"

"Not exactly. You won't be able to bring much of anything into this with you. In fact, I wouldn't even risk writing anything down, until you know what you're dealing with. But…you should be expecting something to be delivered very soon."

Very soon turns out to be *immediately*. Half an hour later when I arrive home to my apartment, I find a wide, narrow garment box waiting for me on my welcome mat. It's taupe and textured—luxury, for sure—with a strange symbol embossed in blood red ink on the top of the box. Broken chain links wrapped around the words *concede voluptati*. A quick search on my phone tells me the Latin words mean *surrender to pleasure*, and a shivering chill licks my spine. I glance both ways down the hall just in case whoever left this here is still lurking around before I snap up the box and dart into my apartment, locking the door behind me.

Concede voluptati. Surrender to pleasure.

I need a new marionette.

Maybe the words should scare me, but the fear is muted by curiosity…and a warm thrill, a buzz low in my abdomen, that I haven't felt in quite some time. At least not without a little battery-powered friend involved. Hell, I'm a workaholic with a job that doesn't even pay well enough to enable alcoholism as a coping mechanism, let alone give me enough free time to *date* anyone. Add to that the thousand and one decisions I have to make on any given day and…surrendering to pleasure sounds *sweet*.

And anyway, whatever this is, it's an audition first and

foremost. I might not even get it.

And if I do? Well…a little pleasure never killed anybody.

This story will continue in His Perfect Plaything…

IF YOU ENJOYED *STORM SOAKED STRANGERS...*

Reviews are insanely powerful for a self-publishing author like me because they help me draw attention to my stories. Someday, I might be lucky enough to have the financial might of a big wig publisher on my side, but for the moment it's just me.

Committed and loyal readers are an amazing gift. Honest reviews help me find other passionate readers, which in turn makes it possible for me to keep writing stories for you all. If you've enjoyed this book, I would be eternally grateful if you could spend just five minutes leaving a review (it can be as short as you like) on whichever platform you purchased this book.

And, if social media's your style, please support me with a follow on Facebook, Instagram, and Pinterest.

Thank you so much!
Xoxo Sierra

ALSO, BE SURE TO CHECK OUT MY OTHER BOOK SERIES

Fantasy Romance

The Garden of Beastly Delights

Billionaire Romance

Revenge & Riches

ABOUT THE AUTHOR

Sierra Prynne is a cheeky little pen name inspired by a run-in with a lovely drunk lady who told me: "You can wake up ten years from now living the life you have or the life you want."

The women in my family have a tradition of using their middle names and Sierra is mine. Prynne is a gift to a certain complex and self-possessed literary character who deserved better. I'm learning about who I want to be as I write these stories and I think she'd respect that.

As for who I am, well, I'm a hopeful romantic who believes you can find true love if you're brave enough not to settle for less than extraordinary. Also, I probably like fantasy a little too much for my own good and when I'm not writing, I can be found wandering through theme parks, national parks, and book parks…those are a thing, right?

You can check out more of what I'm up to at www.sierraprynne.com or email me at sierra@sierraprynne.com.

COPYRIGHT

LURING PRESS

A LURING PRESS book.

First published in the United States in 2025 by LURING
PRESS LLC
Copyright © 2025